God's Riches At Christ's Expense

By Ronnie Daniels

Copyright © 2011 by Ronnie Daniels

God's Riches At Christ's Expense
by Ronnie Daniels

Printed in the United States of America

ISBN 9781613794517

All rights reserved solely by the author. The author guarantees all contents are original and do not infringe upon the legal rights of any other person or work. No part of this book may be reproduced in any form without the permission of the author. The views expressed in this book are not necessarily those of the publisher.

Unless otherwise indicated, Bible quotations are taken from The King James Version.

Cover art by Lisa Clough. To view Lisa's gallery, go to lachri.com

www.xulonpress.com

Contents

Preface vii

Darkness 11

Despised 22

Fallen 33

Fear 42

Promise 50

Forgiven 60

Redeemed 75

Nota Bene 84

PREFACE

While lying in bed one night trying to fall asleep, I was putting the final period to end the events of the present day and preparing to turn the page in commencement of the day to come. At the time, writing was the furthest from my mind. Suddenly without any fore warning, there was an immediate influx of information that began to fill my head. I guess if I had to describe it in contemporary jargon, I would say that it was as if data from a computer was literally being downloaded into my mind.

The first wave of thoughts, were the recollection of stories in the Gospels of the people that Jesus healed. That lasted for several moments as I recalled each of the stories. The second wave that came over me was in the form of a question: Where did these people come from and what were the circumstances of their preceding life that led them to their encounter with Jesus? The third wave was to write their stories.

Wow! First off, the bible is pretty clear in that it does not give too much information in regards to the antedated lives of the people who encountered Jesus and were healed. Second, I definitely did not want to in any way, shape or form; appear to be adding to the word of God. But, if this was a directive coming from the Holy Spirit of God, I wanted to be obedient.

Now obviously I am not a world renowned author, nor am I literary scholar. In fact, I dropped out of college not once, but twice. I guess you would say that I am just an average guy leading an ordinary life. Why would God ask me to write this? I am not sure. Perhaps this is part of my purpose here on Earth.

I believe God created all of us for a specific purpose and that He has bestowed upon us certain gifts. Whether these gifts are of not much significance or grandiose in nature, we have them. It is then our responsibility to choose to act upon and use them as God intended; or we can use them for our own self service and personal gain; or choose to disregard the gifts and not use them at all. Sometimes these gifts are revealed to us, as in my circumstance, via a shift from our normal activity and it is so obvious that we can not ignore it. Other times, the gifts we have may develop and present them selves over time or may be made known to us by others who can perceive our true character. However manner these gifts are divulged, either way, the choice is still ours to whether or not we will apply them in our lives to fulfill our purpose here on Earth. I have chosen to write this with the acceptance that He has given me the gift of writing, although diminutive, still with the intention of fulfilling His purpose of reaching out to many or to a select few.

Each of the following stories is fictional up to the point when they met with Jesus. But I do believe that there may have been a possibility that during each person's path in their journey to healing and restoration, they may have actually experienced some of the same conditions that I wrote about. Inspired by a visit to Israel during the composing of this book, each vignette is unique in that I have incorporated factual sites and authentic historical facts relevant to that era of time. I hope that you appreciate reading this just as much as I enjoyed writing it.

There was an after thought that came later when formatting this book, but I will get into that later on.

DARKNESS

Jesus stood in front of me looking deeply into my eyes. He asked, *"Do you believe in the Son of God?"*

I inquired of him, *"Who is he Lord, that I might believe on him?"*

With the gaze of His eyes piercing my soul, he answered back, *"You have seen him and it is he who is speaking with you."* In that moment before I answered him, I was taken back to a place in time when I was a child in Jerusalem, living with the burden of being blind from birth.

Specifically, I recalled when I was the age of nine and being tenderly cared for by my mother. Because of my disability, I was not allowed to venture too far outside to join the other children in their play. This was due to the fact that I would easily get tripped up and fall. The other children viewed me as clumsy and useless, and would ridicule me. So, for my physical as well as emotional well being, mother kept me confined to home.

I remember sitting in the sweet, tempered breeze just outside my home listening to the other children as they played. The occasional dispute would break out over what game to play. I thought, *'who cares what the game is, at least you get to play'*, and considered how fun it would have been just to join them. But I was destined to sit and listen, a permanent fixture in my solitude.

Mother relieved me of my confinement several times a week by allowing me to accompany her to the market place. She led, while I held tightly to her arm. During one visit, I let go of her arm for a brief moment and was instantly gripped with fear. As the continuous noise of my surroundings closed in around me, I hysterically yelled out for her, grasping at the open air in a frenzied manner. She gently grabbed a hold of my arm and with her soothing voice calmed me down. What was only a brief moment, seemed like an eternity. In spite of that incident, these visits were among my favorite things to do.

The market place's ambience would overload my senses. The aroma of fresh bread baking, the distinct smells of freshly picked fruits and the putrid odor of animal waste filled the air. And the spices! Oh the flavorful fragrance of various spices always stirred up an unquenchable appetite in me.

With my hearing more acute than others, I was more in tune to the conversations going on around me. I would catch discussions about the government, about religion and of course the bartering between merchants and consumers for the best bargain. The atmosphere in the market place was always alive with busy conversations. When my mother was not in too much of a hurry, she would let me feel the different textures of fabrics from far off countries. She did her best to describe the color of the fabrics by associating them with everyday items that I was familiar with. For example, she compared the color yellow to the smell of a freshly picked lemon. She also described the color gray to me as a cool smooth stone that you would find lying on the ground in the shade. But, my favorite description was when she compared the color blue with splashing your face with water on a hot summer day and letting the breeze dry you off. I seemed to learn something new with every visit.

My father worked in a vineyard, tending to the land of a wealthy man. He had been doing this long before I was born and had found favor with his overseer because of his work ethic. He left early in the morning and came home in the evening, always tired. I could tell when he was near, as I would catch a whiff of his redolence as he walked down the path towards our home. He had little time to spend with my mother and me. Since he worked six days a week, the only family time we had together was during the religious holy days and the Sabbaths. The Sabbath day was a time for observance, going to temple, worship and rest. The law restricted anyone from working or doing anything that resembled work, which unfortunately included playing. Although we did not do much on that day, I appreciated what little time we had together.

As I got older, I felt like more of a burden to my family. I did whatever I could to help around our home. I could not find work anywhere and it seemed as though I was of no use to anybody. With the exception of my parents, it appeared that no one cared about my affliction and hardships. This made me to feel dejected and downcast.

Because of my disability, I was reduced to being a beggar, relying on peoples' charity. Even though I felt degraded, I found a place in the city at the edge of a major thoroughfare where I could sit and receive alms. The area I chose was bustling with people while they conducted their daily routine. At the end of each day, I always had some money. Whatever was given to me, I took home and gave it to my mother. This gave me the emotional and moral satisfaction that I was an integral part of supporting my family.

Decades passed and through the years, day in and day out, I sat in the same spot begging. I came to know many of the usual people as they stopped to talk to me and catch me up on the goings on in the region. It was during one of these occasions that I first heard of Him, the man named

Jesus. There was such a buzz about the city concerning him. Stories circulated about him healing people of their infirmities and performing unheard of miracles. His teachings, however, were causing a division among the people. His philosophy seemed to challenge our law. The Pharisees said he was a false prophet, committing blasphemous acts in league with the devil. Others said he was a prophet from God or that he was possibly the Messiah whom we had been waiting for.

Long before, I had heard teachings from the scriptures as to the coming one from God. They taught that the Messiah would overthrow the government and establish His kingdom. I must admit, all of the stories I had heard were interesting, but I was unsure what to think of him. I entertained the thought of him being "The One," but how could he be? Except for the time in the Temple courtyard when he scourged the money changers, he was peaceful and meek. Furthermore, he did not even have an army to overthrow the Romans, rather just a few followers. I would have liked to listen to his teachings while he was in the city; however, unforeseen events in my life deprived me of the chance. Just as in my childhood days, it seemed my fate to miss out on the excitement. It was just as well, the account of his deeds were most likely exaggerated. I once heard of a story propagated by his disciples that he had walked on water. I found that hard to believe. Nonetheless, the accounts of his travels made for good conversation.

Each passing day resembled the last with almost no change, but today was different. It was about midday on the Sabbath when I felt the delicate vibration in the ground pass through my seated body and I sensed something was out of the normal. A short time later, I heard the faint rumble of a large crowd in the distance. People began to rush past me. First there were only a few, then more. There were arousing cries as they charged by, *"He's here, He's here!"* This seemed to touch off hysteria within the city. I rose to my feet and asked what was going on. No one answered me. I yelled out the more, *"Somebody, please tell me what's happening!"* Sensing the proximity of the crowd by the intense escalation of noise, I reached out and caught a hold of a man's coat in my angst.

"I beseech you, tell me what's happening?" I asked in desperation.

The man replied, *"Jesus of Nazareth is come. He is here!"* The man jerked his coat from my grip and I heard him as he hastened off. The excitement was contagious and I could feel enthusiasm begin to swell up in me. I thought, *'Assuredly, this day I will get to hear him teach'*. But, I had to find someone to lead me to his locality within the city. While I stood there considering what to do, I heard the crowd advancing towards me. *'Certainly'*, I thought, *'someone in this horde will have pity on me and direct me to his location'*.

As the throng of people reached me, I overheard one man ask another, *"Master, who did sin, this man or his parents that he was born blind?"* As the other answered him back, I realized that the question pertained to me and that it was Jesus himself who answered. I did not have to go to him, he had come to me. I was overwhelmed with emotion which left me dumbfounded and speechless. I could not believe it, me, a person of least importance had an audience with the man who was possibly the Messiah. With the large crowd now gathered around me and substantially quieted, I heard Jesus bring to a close his answer, *". . . As long as I am in the world, I am the light of the world."* As he finished speaking, there was immediate silence and I eagerly anticipated what would happen next. That's when I heard a soft smack on the ground next to me. Because I was caught unaware by this sudden visitation, my senses were adrift, and I thought he had dropped money in the dirt for me. But, one of the onlookers made it known that Jesus had spit on the ground. I stood baffled and motionless waiting to find out what would happen next.

The moment he touched my face, I knew it was mud from the smell and wet, rough consistency. Then it dawned on me, *'This mud was made from his spit'*. Jesus continued to gently cover my eyes with the mire. When he was done, he told me to go and wash in the pool of Siloam.

An onslaught of thoughts inundated my mind. *'What just happened here? He put mud made of his spit on my eyes and told me to go and wash. This is not what I expected at all. Am I to be the object of ridicule? Is this some cruel joke? Should I be angry or offended by this?'* But there was nobody mocking or laughing at me, just silence. Then I thought, *'Why the pool of Siloam?'* I knew that water from the pool was used for purification rituals in the Temple. *'Is there some significance to this? Can I not just wash my face anywhere?'* I felt the close presence of the assembly that encompassed me and sensed their anticipation to see how I responded to his instructions. Unsure of what to do, I weighed my options.

I do not know why, but a story I had heard long ago came to mind. It was about Naaman, the captain of the host of the king of Syria and his encounter with the prophet Elisha. I remembered that Naaman was given instructions by Elisha to go and wash in the dirty Jordan River seven times to be cleansed of his leprosy. Naaman reluctantly went and did as he was told and because of his obedience, he was cured. There was a reason why Jesus gave me these instructions and like Naaman, I needed to obey.

Without uttering a word, I began to head in the direction of the lower city where the pool of Siloam was located. I did not get too far when a man caught hold of my arm and assisted me on my way. As he led me, many thoughts raced through my doubting but hopeful mind. I then came to the realization that if all the stories about Jesus were true, I would receive my sight. *'Could it be? Will I be able to see?'*

With every moment that passed, my heart beat more powerfully with anticipation to the point where it felt as though my chest was going to burst.

Oh, how my life would change forever. I would be able to see my parents. I would be able to see the trees, animals, sky, the moon and stars. And the colors! All the beautiful colors that had been described to me would come to life. No more tripping and falling or bumping into people. I would be independent and able to work. Maybe have a family of my own. What a precious gift this would be, to be given the world!

I nudged the man to pick up the pace. Finally, after what seemed like an endless trip through the city, he told me, "We are here." He slowly led me down the steps to the edge of the pool where I knelt down and plunged my hands into the cool water. I splashed the water several times onto the now hardened mud that covered my eyes, until it disintegrated. I opened my eye lids, blinking involuntarily and experienced an unfamiliar aching. I had to close and open them several times before I could keep them patent from what I now know was the reflective light of the sun. The first thing I beheld was the palms of my hands as they came into focus. I could see the drops of water mingled with traces of dirt that partially covered the jagged lines. I turned my hands over and examined the dirt in my fingernails and the hair and wrinkles that covered the back of my hands. Then I looked up into the sky at the passing clouds. It was as my mother had described them, *'the wool of sheep moving along in the wind.'* It was beyond anything I had imagined.

I bellowed out, *"I can see! I can see!"* The man, who had led me to the pool, was still at my side. I grabbed him by the shoulders and cried, *"I see!"* He raised his hands up towards the sky and yelled out, *"Praise be to God!"* Due to our exaltation, we continued shouting all the way up the steps leading from the pool. Because of our carrying on, we began to cause a stir and a crowd quickly assembled around us to see what the prattle was about.

After discerning what had just occurred, those in the crowd looked on me with amazement. They debated amongst themselves as to who I was. Some argued that I was the blind man who sat and begged. Others disagreed, saying that I resembled the blind man, but did not think that I was him. I interjected in their dissent and said, *"I am he."* Confused by my statement, they asked how my eyes were opened. I eagerly explained to them, *"The man called Jesus made clay and anointed my eyes with it. He then told me to go and wash in the pool of Siloam. I went and did as he said and washed in the pool and received my sight."* Seeking genuineness to my story, they asked, *"Where is he?"*

I answered back, *"I do not know."*

Bewildered and disputing the account I had just given, they forced me up the road and brought me before the Pharisees. These groups of pious men were the authority on Mosaic Law and had a great deal of influence over the people. As I stood in front of them, a person from the crowd walked over to the faction and had a brief audience with them. After a few moments, they asked me in an accusatory tone, *"How did you receive your sight?"* I briefly reported to them what Jesus had done and said, and how I came to see. Self righteous bickering between them broke out dividing the group into two different factions. One side claimed that Jesus violated the Sabbath by performing this act, and so could not be from God. The counter argument was 'how could a man that is a sinner perform miracles?' This continued back and forth until they reached an impasse. They turned again to me and asked, *"What do you say about him that opened your eyes?"* I ardently replied, *"He is a prophet!"*

Now, the entire crowd began to quibble over the validity of my testimony. A man was sent out to fetch my parents in hopes that they would catch me in a lie and quash the notion of the working of a miracle. I waited with anticipation for my parents to arrive. I was aware that they were going to be informed that I had received my sight, but I also knew they would not believe the report.

When my parents arrived, I recognized my mother from the moment we locked eyes. She was so beautiful! I followed her with my eyes as she passed, and watched as a smile formed, changing her initially perplexed look to one of awe. She realized that there was truth in what they had told her concerning my sight. As she stood before the Pharisees, she turned and looked back at me over her shoulder. I could see the trail of tears rolling down her flushed cheeks. She was enraptured in total elation.

My parents were asked in an indignant tone, *"Is this your son who you say was born blind? How does he now see?"* Because of the influential power the Pharisees had over the people, they chose their words carefully as not to be ostracized and shunned. They timorously answered, *"We know that this is our son, and that he was born blind. But, how he now sees, we know nothing of it or who opened his eyes. He is old enough; ask him, he can speak for himself."*

Again they called me forth and told me to give God the praise and to admit that Jesus was a sinner. But I immediately answered back, *"Whether he is a sinner or not, I do not know. All I know is that I was blind and now I see!"*

In the same, accusatory manner, they asked what Jesus had done and how my eyes received sight. Exasperated at their refusal to believe my answers, I retorted, *"I have told you already and you refuse to hear. Why do you want to hear it again? Will you also be his disciples?"*

Their response was no surprise, they began to curse and insult me. With the same indignant tone as before they shouted at me, *"You are his disciple, but we are Moses' disciples. We know that God spoke to Moses, as for this fellow, we do not know where he is from!"*

I took a deep breath and a sudden peace came over me. I stepped forward and spoke, *"This is remarkable, you don't know where he is from, and yet he has opened my eyes. Now we know that God does not listen to sinners; but if any man is a worshipper of God, and does his will, him he hears. Since the world began nobody has ever heard of any man opening the eyes of one that was born blind. If this man were not from God, he could do nothing!"*

Annoyed and disgusted with my words, they answered back with an explicit charge saying, *"You were altogether born in sins, and you lecture us?"* The congregation became incensed and started to manhandle me, grabbing at my clothes, pushing and shoving all the while denouncing and cursing me. They ultimately forced me out into the street. All I could do was smile. My encounter with them could not diminish the wonderful gift that had been given to me. *"I can see!"* I said out loud to myself. *"I can see!"*

I stood there on the city street taking in every precious sight that my eyes could behold. That's where Jesus had again found me and asked if I believed on him.

Now back in the present, I reverently answered him, *"Lord, I believe!"* and I immediately fell to my knees and worshipped Him.

Jesus said, *"For judgment I am come into this world, that they which see might not see; and they which see might be made blind."*

Now some of the Pharisees were near and had heard what Jesus had said and asked in a brash tone, *"Are we also blind?"*

Jesus replied, *"If you were blind, you should have no sin. But now you say, we see; therefore your sin remains."* They could find no words to answer Him back.

I think what Jesus was saying to the Pharisees is that because of their assertion to have the wisdom, understanding and insight into the spiritual affairs of God, they should have known who He was and believed in him. But, since they were caught up in their own self-righteousness, hardness of heart and ignorance, they did not act upon this knowledge and believe in him; therefore they remain in their sin and remain spiritually blind.

I remembered what I had proclaimed when I was before the Pharisees, *"I was blind, now I see"*. It all made sense. Not only was I physically blind, but I had also been blind to the things of God. I was lost in self-pity and perceived worthlessness. I believed that I was of no good to anyone. But when Jesus found me and opened my eyes, he also opened my heart and showed me that I mattered to him. He made known to me that he loved me for who I was and that my status in life did not matter. He revealed to me that there is a purpose and destiny for my life and whether small or great, that purpose is to bring him glory

DESPISED

I saw Jesus climb to a level place on the hill with his disciples and the multitudes that came after him. Indifferent, yet curious, I followed, making sure to keep my distance. When they reached a certain spot, he turned and began to speak. When he spoke, his voice carried like the wind through the trees interrupted only by the occasional singing bird.

He said, *"Blessed are the poor in spirit: for theirs is the kingdom of heaven. Blessed are they that mourn: for they shall be comforted. Blessed are the meek: for they shall inherit the earth."*

I did not understand his words; *'poor in spirit, those who mourn; the meek inheriting the earth'*, what was he talking about? *'How is that supposed to help me?'* I thought. I did not know which of the reports about him to believe. Was he just a man from Nazareth, the son of a carpenter? Or was he a great teacher from God? Did he really heal the sick? Why did others say he was a deceiver giving false hope to people? Confused by these conflicting stories, I turned as he continued to speak and looked out over the Sea of Galilee. I watched as the local fishermen from Capernaum hauled nets, laden with fish, into their boats. I saw the sunlight shimmer upon the waves and felt the breeze as it wafted across the water. I recalled traveling to this area as a boy with my father.

Those were much simpler times. I would give anything to step back into that time when life was not so complicated.

As a boy, my father would often bring me with him as he delivered his wares to the surrounding area. He was a master carpenter with a reputation for making the finest furnishings and equipment in the region. He had received his training as a young man living in Jerusalem. His craft had been acquired from the same master carpenters who had trained the Levites who worked on the construction of Herod's Temple. He had even worked on some of the outlying gates of the city making repairs and improvements.

After five years spent mastering his trade, he married my mother and soon after she gave birth to my sisters. They lived in Jerusalem until my sisters reached the ages of five and four. Then, with the political environment in upheaval and the ever looming threat of tumult, my family left Jerusalem and relocated north to the city of Sephoris overlooking the plains of Samaria in the region of Galilee. The aggregation of crops, coupled with fishing commerce from the Sea of Galilee made this one of the richest provinces in the Empire.

Having settled in a new principality, my father was in want of having a son to whom to teach his trade. His desire was fulfilled when I was born. As soon as I was able to walk and hold tools, I regularly accompanied him to his work place in the city. My mother, thinking that I was too young maintained that I should stay home with her while she ground grain, baked bread and performed her daily chores. But, my father's aphorism was *'If you do not teach your son how to work, you teach him how to be a thief'*.

The shop where he worked was a single room with one window. It was filled with all manner of tools. The front door faced the market place and was directly across from the black smith. The two shops were strategically placed, since many of the implements my father made required metal parts and, of course the opposite was true as well.

My father acquainted me with the different types of wood he liked to work with, including acacia and cypress. For carving decorations he used olive wood which had a deep luster to it. After familiarizing me with the various types of wood, he introduced me to the proper use of his assorted tools. There were so many.

I learned how to use several different axes and saws to chop wood and make precise cuts. He showed me how cut against the grain to produce a choice piece of wood to work with. I was taught how to use the vice and cane bender for furniture and work implements that had arched or circular shapes. I was shown how to drill precise holes using a bow with string wrapped around a sharpened piece of iron and how to smooth the wood using different types of rubbing stones.

Because wood was expensive, my father ingrained in me the importance of looking at every piece of wood, small or large, as being potentially promising rather than focusing on any of the imperfections that it may have had in it. He trained me to be highly disciplined and honed my skills in order not to waste any wood.

Because the region bustled with an abundance of farms, there was a constant demand for farming implements such as yokes, plows, rakes and axles for olive presses. I watched my father as he built each apparatus with speed and brilliance. Each item he produced was flawless. I was about six years of age when he first allowed me to start helping him with the construction of these implements.

After he had completed a certain number of these tools, he would pack them up on our donkey and he and I would set out to the farms surrounding the Sea of Galilee. After he sold all of the articles to the farmers, we would visit the city of Tiberius. There we would take in the sights, go fishing and eat exotic foods. These trips usually lasted three to four days and I enjoyed every moment.

God's Riches At Christ's Expense

At ten I had my first solo undertaking, making a threshing sledge for the cornfields of a nearby farmer. Patiently, I made sure every piece fit together perfectly and every drilled hole was precise. It took me almost a month to complete the task, but my efforts paid off. The day we delivered the sledge to the farmer I was anxious to see if it would work properly. We watched as he harnessed the sledge to his oxen then led him over the corn stalks. It worked perfectly, separating the husks. My father stood and held his head high, filled with pride. I was overflowing with a sense of accomplishment. I found it difficult to curb my enthusiasm and I could not wait to get back to the shop and build something new.

My mother believed that as a young boy, I should not be working all the time, rather going to synagogue to receive an education and to learn about my heritage. But my father, who had been educated, insisted that he would teach me everything that I needed to know, and he did.

Although we obeyed the Law, observing the Holy days and the Sabbath, my father was not a very religious man. He thought that only the weak minded and insecure needed religion in their lives. Because of this we went to the synagogue only a handful of times when I was growing up. It was just as well, I was so enthralled with carpentry, that it slowly consumed my life. In a time when I should have been playing with the other children, I was busy at work constructing my future.

As I matured into a young adult, my father relinquished more and more responsibility to me as my knowledge and ability expanded. I accepted each task as a challenge, always with the purpose to make my father proud.

Over time, the region's population grew with an influx of people to the area, and the need for land increased. Every week more people migrated to Sephoris and the surrounding towns. The expansion of cities resulted in the loss of available rural farming areas. With it, the bid for farming implements also decreased. However these growing communities placed their own demands in relation to carpentry items. People needed tables, chairs, roofing and doors for the homes. Even the fishermen needed sailing masts, oars and rudders for their fishing boats. My father and I were busier than we had ever been and were having difficulty keeping up with the demands. Because we were so overwhelmed, we had to send people to the carpenters that resided in the neighboring cities of Cana and Nazareth.

During this busy period in my life, I married a beautiful woman from my city and as time passed, we also had two daughters. Like my father, I too longed to have a son to mentor in the art of carpentry. Despite the absence of a son, my life was good and I was taking great pleasure in it. But different seasons bring change and my life was no exception to the rule. My father, now an old man, became ill and within a month's time, he died. This appeared to be the catalyst that sent my life into a downward spiral.

One day, not long after my father had passed, I was working in the shop and noticed that there was a red rash about half the size of a finger nail on my right forearm near the elbow. At first I thought nothing of it, assuming that I must have brushed against a piece of wood and scratched it. But when the rash failed to go away in a week's time, I became a little worried. I showed the rash to my wife and she immediately admonished me to go to the synagogue and consult the Rabbi. Though I was apprehensive to what he would tell me, I went to go see him anyway.

The Rabbi examined the rash and informed me that I would have to be isolated for an entire week at which time he would re-examine me. I was reluctant to be isolated from my family and work for a week, but he persuaded me by assuring me that it would protect my family from possible contamination of any contagious disease.

I followed the advice of the Rabbi, but on my own terms. I remained secluded in my closed shop for a week. To help pass the time, I made small carvings of different animals that I planned to give to my daughters. The only contact I had with any one was when my wife came to leave me food and drink at the door. As the week progressed, I noticed that the rash on my arm had grown in size and knew that this was not a good sign.

Finally, after the week had passed, I revisited the Rabbi. As he was examining my rash, he let out a big sigh and said, *"My son, I have to declare you unclean. You have the leprosy."*

I just stood there staring at him not believing what he had just told me. After a few agonizing moments, I said, *"Rabbi, you must be mistaken. Please check it again and make sure."*

"My son," he answered, *"I have diagnosed many with the leprosy. Your rash has grown and is now under your skin and the hairs on the rash have turned white. There is no doubt. You have the leprosy."*

I was stunned and filled with disbelief. Deep down I knew he was telling me the truth, but I did not want to believe it. My heart became heavy and tears began to form in my eyes as I thought of my family and what would become of them. Attempting to console me he said, *"My son, when a person is stricken with this sort of disease, it is because they have in some way sinned against God. But let me assure you that there also is healing within the hand of God. Examine yourself and seek out this sin and atone for it."*

Angrily I lashed out at him, *"I have not sinned. All my life I have worked hard. I have loved my family and treated no one dishonestly. If God is going to punish me like this, then he is nothing more than a cruel God and I do not want his help!"* I violently charged out of the synagogue and went back to my shop.

I arrived at my shop, still in total denial of my current circumstances. I grabbed a smoothing stone, dipped it in water and vigorously scoured the rash, desperately trying to scrub it off my arm. I only succeeded in rubbing my arm raw. I sat there for hours staring at the ground full of self pity, contemplating how my disease would impact my family's life.

When my wife brought me my meal in the evening, she assumed that everything was better and started to make her way through the door. I yelled at her to stop. When she saw the look on my face, she immediately knew that something was wrong. Holding back my tears, I told her the bad news. She fell to the ground and wept. I just looked at her from across the room incapable of offering any consolation. I so desperately wanted to go to her and hold her in my arms.

On account of my disease, I could not go home nor could I stay at the shop in the market place. In accordance with the law, the only option I had was to live outside of the city, separated from everyone. I waited for nightfall and using the cover of darkness to avoid contact with anyone, I took as many tools as I could carry and went into the hillside a short distance from the main thoroughfare. I used my tools to help construct a small, comfortable shelter to live in. Due to a lack of financial support and sustenance, my wife and daughters were forced to move back in with her parents to ensure their survival.

My days were long and lonely and consisted mostly of trying to gather food. Every now and then during my foraging I would happen upon other people. When it looked like we were going to make contact with each other, I had to cover my mouth and state *'unclean, unclean'* as a warning to them that I was diseased. It was contemptible the way they behaved towards me. I was shunned and treated like an outcast. The only thing that lifted my spirits was when my wife and daughters came to visit. During our visits, they always kept a safe distance between us. Not having physical contact with them became more and more emotionally difficult for all of us to bear.

The visits from my family became less and less frequent as the months passed. After about a year's time, my loneliness intensified when they stopped coming by altogether. Compounding my already low spirits, I began to notice that the disease was aggressively manifesting itself on my body. My skin hardened and was very dry. Lesions developed on my elbows, knees, and buttocks. I noticed that in the areas where the lesions were, there was a decrease in sensitivity to touch. My nasal cavity was constantly dry and I had frequent nose bleeds. My muscles weakened which made it difficult at times to walk or pick up things.

One day while fetching water at a nearby stream, I came to realize how far the leprosy had advanced when I saw my reflection in the water. I gasped at the sight of my severely disfigured face. My nose had lost its shape and was now just a massive clump. My eyebrows and eyelashes were nearly nonexistent and there were lesions scattered about my entire face. I now knew why my wife and daughters would no longer visit me; I was hideous to look upon. Filled with despair and with no further reason to stay in the area, I abandoned my camp and began to roam aimlessly through the countryside.

In my wonderings through the back roads, I came across other lepers who were also living as outcasts. Although their companionship was duly needed, I did not remain in their company long as the site of them was a crude reminder of my own hopeless situation. One afternoon, I happened upon a small group of lepers living collectively in a primitive, make shift village. They bid me to lodge with them for the evening. Weary from traveling all day, I accepted their invitation and stayed.

It was during the evening, while we were gathered around the fire, that I heard the different reports about Jesus.

Although those in the camp had not personally encountered him, you could sense their excitement as they shared stories that they had heard. Some related that he was the Son of God and had healed many of the sick and afflicted. Others voiced the opinion that he was a fraud. Their argument was that he was an activist trying to gain support and stir the people up against the Roman government. What caught my attention was when one of the men mentioned that Jesus came from Nazareth and was the son of a carpenter. I thought, *'could this be the same carpenter whose name was Joseph?'* During the occasional travels with my father when I was younger, I had met a carpenter from Nazareth named Joseph who had many sons and daughters. Unsure what to make of all this, I kept my thoughts to myself and just listened as they rambled on. When I awoke early in the morning, I picked up my belongings and left the encampment while the others slept.

As I traveled along the north shore of the Sea of Galilee, I could see a large multitude of people gathered in the short distance ahead on the side of a hill that overlooked the lake. Looking around, I saw others coming from all directions moving like a brood of insects, all heading towards the same hill. Curious to what was happening, I shouted out to a group heading towards the hill, *"Please, tell me where you are going?"*

One man shouted back, *"We are going to see Jesus there on the hill."*

I thought, *'so he does exist; he is not a myth. I will go see what he is about.'*

I ambled towards the bottom of the hill where I was able to catch a glimpse of Jesus in the distance. He did not look the way I thought he would. He was dressed in simple clothing and his appearance was one of submissiveness. This was not quite the likeness of someone who was supposed to be the Son of God. Yet, there was something about him that was enthralling and intriguing. I waited to hear what he had to say.

And now, standing at the bottom of the hill, not understanding his words and no better off, I thought what a waste of my time it had been to come here. I turned and walked along the shore away from the hill.

As I walked, I looked ahead into the empty countryside and realized that I had no place to go and nothing else to do. I thought to myself, *'what could it possibly hurt to hear what he had to say.'*

I turned around and walked the short distance back to where I was previously standing and resumed listening to him:

"Not every one that says unto me Lord, Lord, shall enter into the kingdom of heaven; but he that does the will of my Father which is in heaven. Many will say to me in that day, Lord, Lord, have we not prophesied in your name? And in your name have cast out devils? And in your name done many wonderful works? And I will profess to them, I never knew you: Depart from me, you that work iniquity."

Jesus continued, *"Therefore whoever hears these sayings of mine, and does them, I will liken him unto a wise man, which built his house upon a rock: And the rain fell, and the floods came, and the winds blew and beat upon the house; and it did not fall for it was founded on a rock. And everyone that hears these sayings of mine and does not do them, shall be likened unto a foolish man, which built his house upon the sand: The rain fell, the floods came, and the winds blew, and beat upon that house; and it fell: and great was the fall of it."*

I began to relate to what he was talking about. I had worked on many houses and had seen what happens when those with weak foundations are exposed to turbulent weather. However, he was not talking about houses; he was referring to something more meaningful, he was speaking in reference to the foundation that one's life is built upon. As I continued to ponder his sayings, I was cut deeply to the heart. I realized that my entire life was built on a shoddy foundation based on the temporal things of this world. I had rejected and exiled God from my life much like the way I had been shunned and despised by others. I had forsaken Him from my life and in turn He gave me what I wanted, a life absent of Him.

His words, *"I never knew you: Depart from me, you that work iniquity"* echoed over and over in my head and I was overcome with fear. I had become conscious of the fact that I was a sinner and fearful that I would never be able to get my life in order. And when my time for judgment came, I knew that he would speak those very words to me, casting me from his presence forever. I wondered, *'Would He ever forgive me for my obstinacy?'*

Jesus finished speaking and headed down the hill as the multitudes followed. As he reached the bottom of the hill, I went to him, fell to my knees and worshipped him. With repentance in my heart and conscious of the need to be cleansed from the inside out, I said, *"Lord, if you will, you can make me clean."*

Jesus reached out, touched me and said, *"I will; be thou clean."*

Immediately there was a rush of power that overwhelmed my body. When I looked down at my arms and hands, the leprosy was gone and my skin was smooth. I was made whole again. Jesus then said to me, *"See that you tell no man; but go your way and show yourself to the priest and offer the gift that Moses commanded, for a testimony unto them."*

I departed to go and do as I was instructed, and realized that I had been relieved of the fear that had once gripped me. He had granted me forgiveness and favor far beyond what I could never earn. My fear had been replaced by the love of God and the assurance of salvation.

FALLEN

I stood at the entrance to the house and saw the silhouette of a man sitting at a table. I waited for my eyes to adjust from the outside sunlight to the darkness that lay within. As my eyes adjusted, I could see the figure more clearly as he fully came into view. He was an older man with long gray hair and a beard to match. His clothing was dark gray and he had parchments laid out on the table in front of him.

I enquired, *"Is this the house of Jotham the physician?"*

He replied, *"It is and I am he. Come in."*

I immediately answered back, *"I am unclean."*

"Usually those who come to see me are! Please come in," he retorted in a matter of fact tone.

I entered and stood near the table. The stale smell of the room instantly filled my nose and repulsed me.

"What can I do for you?" he asked in a scratchy monotone voice.

Trying to hold back the tears, all I could invoke was, *"I need you to . . . I am . . . there is no one who can . . . I am diseased with . . ."* I then began to sob uncontrollably.

He stood, grabbed a chair and placed it at the table and implored me to sit down.

As I sat, I choked back my tears and attempted to explain my plight, *"I was told that you might possibly be able to help me. I have tried everything. Nothing is helping. I am so tired of looking for . . ."* he abruptly stopped me.

Then he requested, *"Please, start from the beginning so that I can better understand."*

I took a few deep breaths and collected my thoughts. After a few moments I was able to give him an account of my travails.

"My story goes back thirteen years and starts in the city of Scythopolis of the region of Decapolis, near where the Jordan River and Jezreel Valley come together. I lived just outside the city with my parents who were poor, owning little. My father tended to an olive grove that was nearly an hour's walk away. My mother was impaired in one of her legs, limiting the amount of work she could do. The owner of the olive grove where my father worked did not pay much, so I was obligated to help. To assist in supplementing our household income, I found work tending sheep and milking goats at a small farm owned by another family. The farmer paid me in goat's milk which I was able to sell or trade for food at the city market place.

My daily routine consisted of getting up before sunrise and completing the household chores. I made sure my mother was taken care of, and then I would leave for the farm. After half the day attending to the animals at the farm, I would carry my payment of goat's milk in two small pots and walk into the city. Since the city was the capital of the region, it was always busy with activity, so it did not take long for me to sell or trade the milk. In a week I could make up to three dinars which was about half of my father's weekly salary. I would then buy what food I could, bring it home and help prepare the meal.

While traveling between the marketplace and home, I would pass the bath house where the affluent men would spend their time exercising and socializing. That's where I caught the eye of a frequent attendee to the bath house, the son of a wealthy land owner. He began courting me and, from time to time, would walk with me a short distance as I traveled home. Occasionally, he would sit with me in the market place while I sold the milk.

One evening, several months later, he came to my home to speak with my father. I overheard their conversation and learned that he was seeking my hand in marriage. They were bartering over a dowry to be paid to my father. The dowry was to compensate my family's loss of income that they would incur when I left. They came to an accord: One hundred and fifty shekels, equal to nearly two years of my father's salary, one ram and two goats. This was a great amount to be paid for a dowry and it pleased my father.

I was betrothed to him for eight months. When the day of our wedding arrived, my mother and the other young local women helped me prepare during the day. When evening arrived, the young women and I sat in my parents' home, waiting in anticipation for my groom to arrive.

When I heard music in the distance, I knew he was approaching and my heart began to race. The young women and I lit our lamps and waited for my groom to knock at the door. The sound of his light raps on the wood invigorated me and I darted towards the entryway to open the door. There he stood, adorned in a beautiful light blue colored robe and coat with golden linings and an extravagant garland that matched the one I had on over my veil. He gently reached out for my hand. I stepped through the threshold and placed my hand in his; beginning our procession to the home we were to share. Upon reaching our home to be, we saw all the guests and Rabbi waiting for us. We stood before the Rabbi and exchanged our wedding vows. After the completion of our vows, he blessed us and we were presented as husband and wife. All of our guests stood and cheered for us marking the beginning of the celebration feast. The feast lasted seven days and was replete with music, the finest food and much wine.

We began our lives together with hopes of immediately starting a family. When I missed my first menstruation, I became excited, believing that I had conceived, but my excitement would soon turn to trepidation. Just two months after our wedding I had my first discharge. The discharge continued irregularly for several weeks. Because of this, I was deemed unclean and had to live separately from my husband until the time where I could be purified. However, my bleeding did not cease. The issue continued off and on without relenting. At first my husband was patient and understanding, but I saw his patience turn to frustration and disappointment.

This cycle continued for several more months and I became weak and my spirit distressed. I sought the advice of local mid-wives for a cure. One recommended the use of mandrakes, better known as 'love plants'. She advised me that they were used as a remedy for infertility and might offer me relief. When I could muster enough strength, I searched the nearby countryside for the distinct whitish-green flowered plant bearing the orange and red berries. I came across several of the plants and dug up the parsnip shaped root and went home. I consumed the roots for two weeks in every way possible. I ate them raw, boiled, cooked over an open flame, and even tried drinking them in tea, but my bleeding continued as before.

I went to the synagogue and sought guidance from the Rabbi. I was aware that he had some knowledge of the various symptoms of disease and sicknesses and could possibly help. To my disappointment, he insisted that my plight was the result of sin or some direct disobedience to God. He declared me ritually unclean, and advised me to remain separate from the rest of the community until I was clean. I recognized that, as a spiritual leader, it was his duty to help preserve the community and prevent contamination to others. I cried all the way home. I continued to visit the synagogue regularly for help, but nothing changed, the bleeding persisted.

One afternoon my husband came home accompanied with the Rabbi. They approached and stopped in front of me. My husband extended his right hand towards me and I observed that it held a rolled up parchment. He gestured for me to take it. Not fully understanding what was happening, I reached out and he dropped the parchment into my hand. He then stated, *"This is your 'Get', accept this as your 'Get', you shall now be divorced from me. You are untied, free and permitted to any man."* My eyes welled up with tears and they streamed down my cheeks. I stood immobile, only able to stare into his eyes. I could not believe that he was divorcing me. It had come to the point that because of my continued bleeding. He had found me unclean and I had fallen out of favor with him. I thought of the process he had to go through earlier in the day to obtain the 'Get'. He had to go before the Rabbi, find two witnesses, have the scribe write up the 'Get', and then have the witnesses sign it. I was sure that everyone in the city would now know of my misfortune. This was shameful for me and my family.

I could not lawfully oppose this; it was in accordance with the law and I had no choice but to complete the ritual. I placed the 'Get' under my arm and turned away. Moving away a few steps, I returned and handed it to the Rabbi who then tore the 'Get'. As I continued to sob, the Rabbi handed me a divorce certificate and, just like that, after four months, our marriage was dissolved.

My now former husband bestowed some compassion on me. Before leaving what was once our home, he gave me fifty shekels so I would not leave destitute. My life of solitude only became worse from that point on. I was tainted and could not have any close association with other people. Any contact with others would cause them to be ritually unclean. If anyone strayed too close to me, I would have to announce the words, "unclean, unclean" as a warning to them. I could not even have close contact with my parents.

I put up a small tent on the outskirts of town not far from my parents' home. I did not have to spend much money; my parents helped me by periodically leaving food and supplies near my tent. Other times, I foraged in the fields and collected what I could. I primarily used my money to pay the different physicians from the surrounding area for treatments I received for my ailment.

I lived in the same tent, facing adversity and solitude for nearly five years. From time to time when I found the strength, I ventured into the surrounding villages in search of a cure for my ailment, with no success. I finally realized that if I was to find a true cure, I would need to journey to other cities to find a good physician. I packed up what few belongings I had, said goodbye to my parents and traveled south to the city of Pella.

In Pella, I found several physicians who assured me that they could help, but insisted that it would take time for their potions to work effectively. They used ancient remedies involving the use of various herbs and ground up root cuttings. Over the next several years I ate and drank different potions and rubbed ointments on my body, but nothing worked.

I then headed north to the city of Gadara where I found an eccentric physician who also promised he could help me. After examining me he attributed my ailment to evil spirits. He used the heart, gall and liver of a fish and burnt them like incense all around my body. He combined this with incantations all with the purpose of chasing away the evil spirits that he believed caused my disease. This also failed to work.

I finally ended up here in Nahum still searching for relief. For the past twelve years, my issue of blood has continued to drain me not only of my life but also of all my money. I have spent all that I had trying to find a cure. I have nothing left and I am desperate. Will you please help me?"

Intrigued, but yet somewhat indifferent, Jotham sat there silent while mulling over the story I had just chronicled. Then he spoke, *"I am a physician that is true. I can prescribe different herbs and roots for some sicknesses but they are no different than what has already been administered to you. The person whom you seek is a prophet of God, not a man of medicine. I can do nothing to bring you relief. I am sorry, I cannot help you."*

Disheartened, I stood, walked to the doorway, turned to him and flippantly said, *"No such person exists. No one can help me."*

I exited the house and ambled towards the edge of the village.

The sight of a large crowd gathered around a single man caught my attention. My curiosity piqued, I approached, while careful to maintain some distance. I overheard a partial conversation between two men, *". . . He is truly of God!"*

I inquired of them from a distance, *"Who is of God?"*

One man replied, *"Jesus."*

"Who is Jesus?" I asked.

"You do not know who Jesus is? Where are you from?" He retorted.

"Tell me why do you say that he is from God?" I asked.

"He has done many great things. He has healed the sick and lame. He has cast devils out of many. Only God can do such things!" He enthusiastically replied.

I responded, *"No man can heal another. It is impossible!"*

"I tell you we have seen these things happen with our very own eyes!" He exclaimed.

I pointed to the man the group was gathered around and asked, *"Is that him sitting on the rock?"*

"Yes."

'Could this be possible?' I thought to myself. I made my way towards him, pushing aside the crowd as I moved forward. I was supposed to announce my uncleanness and I should not have been touching anybody, but I felt hope rising in me and I had to reach him. Just before I reached him, a man ran up, fell to his knees and began to worship Jesus. The man besought Jesus saying, *"My little daughter lies at the point of death; I pray thee, come and lay your hands on her, that she may be healed and she shall live."*

Jesus arose and went with the man. After hearing the stories, seeing the man fall to his knees in worship and seeing Jesus' reaction to the man's appeal, a newfound faith was born in me and I believed that he was truly of God. I also believed that not only would he heal the little girl, but could heal me as well

As Jesus followed the man, the crowd also pressed around him, closing my path to Him. My faith in Him had over ridden any fear of consequence of breaking the law and I pushed and shoved people with all of my strength to get to Him. Just as I came within arms' reach, I was pushed down to the ground and fell to my knees directly behind Him. Certain that He would soon be out of my reach; I thought *'If I could just touch the hem of his garment, I will be made whole'*. I reached out and grabbed a hold of the hem of his robe. Immediately there was a rush of power and warmth that filled my entire body. I felt my strength instantaneously renewed within me. I knew I had been healed. I sat there soaking up this wonderful vitality, not wanting the moment to end.

Just then, Jesus stopped and said, *"Who touched me?"*

One of his disciples answered, *"Master, the throng is all about you pressing in and you ask who touched you?"*

Jesus said, *"Somebody has touched my clothes, I felt power leave my body."*

Hearing His words, the crowd moved aside exposing my position. When He looked at me, I began to tremble in fear over what I had done. I was not allowed to be around people, let alone touching them. The very act would make them ritually unclean. I knelt before him and explained why I had touched his robe. Jesus looked at me, smiled and with loving compassion in his voice said, *"Daughter, be of good comfort; your faith has made you whole. Go in peace."*

After the many years of futile searching in my fallen state, I realized that it was my belief in Him, the infallible truth of God which brought me to redemption. Not only was I made physically whole, but He had restored my soul.

FEAR

A blood curdling scream in the distance grabbed my attention and caused me to open my eyes. As another scream rang out, I realized that it was I who was screaming, but I was not in control. Much to my horror, my nightmare was still continuing.

As I lay in a fetal position next to the tombs, the odor of decaying bodies filled the air. I could see the dawn starting to break over the hill, revealing a clear sky. And for just a moment, there was peace. Then the tormenting of my mind and body renewed itself much like it had during the days and nights before. Wave after convulsing wave shook my body uncontrollably and every muscle burned and felt as if it were being turned inside out. The voices taunted louder and louder, yelling curses, making my head feel as though it would burst open at any moment. I tried to stand and resist, but the pain worsened and my suffering continued. I was violently thrown to the ground and blacked out.

When I came to, I was looking up at the noonday sun. The smell of the dead was no longer present and I could hear the faint sound of crashing waves. I had somehow been relocated from near the tombs to near the shore of the Sea of Galilee with no memory of what had happened in between. The controlling power of demonic activity had ceased for the moment and I breathed cautiously. I looked over my shoulder at the hill where my home city of Gadera sat and desperately longed to be there.

Gadera was the city where I was born and raised with my brothers. Just like our father, we were fisherman of the Sea of Galilee. At an early age our father taught us the skills needed to carry out our trade. We first learned about the different types of nets that were used and the fishing methods associated with each net. When the men went out to sea, our father made us stay behind on the shore. We built small fires and waited for them to return. When the nets were hauled in, we would gather a basket of fish and cook them for the men to eat when they were done working. This was my favorite time. While they were gathered around the fire eating, the men would tell stories of fabled magical fish that they had encountered or of various sea creatures lurking in the depths. I was attentive to each detail and always wanted to hear more. When we got older, we were introduced to the sailing boats. We learned how to sail and maneuver them through the waters and were shown the best locations on the lake to catch fish.

When I matured into a young man, I became part of a fishing crew that worked the dragnets. Working with the dragnets required a lot of strength and stamina, but the emphasis was on team work. If everyone did not do their share pulling in the nets, the fish would easily escape. The net we used was wide, long and very heavy. We would sail out several hundred cubits from shore, drop and spread out our nets then slowly drag them to shore. Hundreds of fish would get trapped as the nets were drug along the bottom. This method took the longest but yielded the most fish.

I enjoyed night time fishing the most. We usually started in the early evening just as the sun was setting and the cool breezes began blowing across the water. We would sail to the warm springs of Tabgha on the north shore. This was a prime location for night fishing. We would always catch hundreds of fish consisting mostly of Tilapia. Every now and again I would catch a glimpse of a solitary naked fisherman on the shore using a cast net. Because he had to wade into the water to throw his net, he would leave his clothes on shore so that he would have something dry to wear on the way home. I built many fond memories during this time I spent fishing with my father and brothers.

Over time, my brothers married and started their own families. Because of the demand placed on them by their newly formed families, they stopped fishing all together and formed a new livelihood of selling fish in the marketplace. This opened up several spots in our crew that needed to be filled. Eventually these positions were filled by several experienced fishermen who had recently moved to our village from the city of Caesarea. Because of their hard work and skill, they proved to be an asset to the crew.

One night while we were on the shore collecting the fish from our nets, Jambres, one of the new crew members, found an all white fish and became agitated. He exclaimed, *"This is a bad omen!"* and immediately tossed the fish back into the lake. Apparently disturbed, he pulled out a stone he had on a necklace around his neck and kissed it several times. He carefully placed the stone back and continued gathering fish.

Later that evening when we were gathered around the fire eating, I asked Jambres to explain his earlier actions in regard to the white fish. He admonished me that, *"There is more to our world than just us. There is also the spirit world that we have to contend with. When we were gathering the fish, I noticed that the white fish was the only one of its kind in the net. It was not normal. When something like this occurs, it is a sign from the spirits that we are encroaching into their realm without giving them respect. If we do not honor them, something bad is going to happen. If we would have kept the fish, something bad would have befallen us. I returned it so that order would be maintained."*

I asked, *"What about that thing around your neck?"*

He pulled out the stone and said, *"This, my friend is an amulet. It offers me protection and keeps away evil spirits."* He went on to explain to me that there were evil spirits all around and that we required the protection of good spirits. My curiosity was aroused by what Jambres was telling me and I wanted to hear more. He continued on, expounding to me how I needed to open my mind to the good spirits so I could receive their protection. The more I heard the more intrigued I became. Finally, after hours of talking, we parted ways.

In the following nights, he disclosed more and more information until I entreated him to help me open up my mind. Happy to oblige me, he presented me with an amulet to wear around my neck that was similar to his. He then taught me several incantations to recite while holding it and said that it would offer me protection. I was excited by the prospect of evolving in this new found faculty and my passion for its benefits was becoming unquenchable.

One night after fishing when everybody else had gone home, Jambes offered me a drink of potion made from a mixture of acacia tree and herbs. He assured me that it would help me relax and free up my spirit. I was hesitant at first, but after he drank some, I gave in and had several gulps. The drink was bitter and dry like a bad wine. Upon consuming the potion, I noticed an almost immediate effect. The feeling that came over me was capricious in nature. First I felt warm and tremendously relaxed. Then I felt as though I was weightless and floating. The shadows moved about like tiny people tiptoeing across the sand trying to avoid the incoming waves on the shore. The stars in the sky came alive, joined up with the flickering flames and danced like lightening in the heavens. My skin felt as if it was crawling about my entire body. I heard indistinct voices all around me, but there was no one but Jambes. Even though the experience was somewhat unnerving, it was something new and enchanting like nothing I had ever felt before.

In my mind this was an unexplored existence and I thought it divine. My longing to relive this experience found me drinking the potion more frequently. Over time this newly developed appetite gave way to self- indulgence. Drinking wine in excess became commonplace and my inability to control these habits in my life began to take their toll. I rarely showed up to fish and my sleep was constantly disrupted by nightmares that left me gasping for breath and drenched in sweat. I began hearing voices and felt as though I was being prodded by invisible beings. These events would occur even when I did not consume the potion. There was a definite transformation that was occurring in my life and it was not for the better. I was slowly losing control of my will.

One night, after several months of increasingly vile behavior, Jambes convinced me that I was under attack by evil spirits. He persuaded me that I needed to contact the spirit world to harness their powers and make them work to my advantage. He led me to an area next to the tombs and built a small fire. We sat down next to it and began to repeatedly chant a prayer he said would summon the spirits.

For a moment there was an eerie stillness in the air, and then it happened. It felt as though a large boulder had crashed on top of me. Immediately I was displaced to another dwelling where I could not discern time. I was falling in an empty darkness that had no end. This darkness was somehow alive and had completely enveloped my soul. I experienced loss, hopelessness, anguish and tremendous grief. The only thing that I could perceive was that I seemed to be plummeting deeper and deeper into the vast expanse of an unseen abyss.

I do not know how long I was falling in this darkness, but when I resurfaced into our world, it was daylight and I was lying in an open field being bound with rope by four of the men from town. As I looked around in my confused state, I noticed that I was naked with cuts and bruises all over my body.

I yelled at the men, *"What are you doing? Where are my clothes? Untie me now!"*

One of the men responded back, *"After what you did in town last night, we are taking you to the authorities!"*

"What are you talking about? Untie me now!" I barked out. Ignoring me, they continued tying me up. Looking over my wounds, I yelled out, *"Why did you do this to me?"*

Another answered back, *"You did this to yourself!"*

Curious and now somewhat quieted, I asked, *"What are you talking about?"*

Then one of the men confronted me in an accusatory tone, *"You do not remember last night when you ran through town half dressed hollering at the top of your lungs? You knocked down the pen fencing in a man's goats setting them free. Then you knocked down the door of a house, entered, smashed all the dishes and pots and attacked the inhabitants. Then you tried to do the same at another house but could not gain entry and ran off. Were you drunk or are you just mad? Either way, you will have to pay!"*

"I did no such thing! You must be mista . . ." I was interrupted when my voice was compulsively closed up by a mounting force within my body. My eyes burned and rolled back into my head and I could feel a pool of saliva foam up inside my mouth. A surge of strength welled in my body causing the muscles in my chest, arms and legs to swell. As it reached the crescendo, I snapped the ropes tied around my arms and legs like they were dried twigs and rose to my feet. The men quickly advanced and attempted to subdue me, but their efforts proved fruitless. Within moments, I had knocked them all to the ground with tremendous force and departed in a mad sprint while emitting a horrible shriek. Through the entire incident I had no control and seemed to

be shackled with a heavy burden of anguish and pain. I was living in a boundless, violent nightmare.

Night after day and day after night, I continued to terrorize the town. On occasion I would attack people and at other times destroy property. I faded in and out of consciousness sometimes recalling certain events, and yet there would be other occasions when I would wake up in unfamiliar places unaware of how I came to be there. I awoke one morning bound by chains and the next thing I remembered, I was running loose through the orchards in the hills. I frequented the tombs and burial grounds invariably surrounded by death though certainly not by choice. At times when the emptiness would overwhelm me, I would use sharp rocks to cut my body so I could feel something. While at other times, I would wake up already being severely injured. My miserable existence was worse than that of a rabid animal. And now I sat here near the shore of the lake where I had once loved to fish wondering how long must I suffer in this torment.

At that moment I saw a small ship that had made its way towards a nearby embankment and those on board preparing to come ashore. As the men in the ship alighted, I was compelled by the force within me to run towards them. As I reached the leader of the group, I was constrained to bow down in front of him.

My mouth opened and I heard my altered coarse voice speak to him, *"What have I to do with you, Jesus, the Son of the most high God? I adjure you by God that you torment me not."*

The Jesus replied, *"Come out of the man you unclean spirit. What is your name?"*

The voice from within me answered back, *"My name is legion, for we are many. Please do not send us into the abyss. Send us into the swine that we may enter them."*

Jesus told them to go and at his command, the heavy burden was lifted from me and I felt life flood into my body and soul. I heard a nearby herd of pigs squeal uncontrollably and when I looked up I beheld the entire group run off a cliff into the lake and drown.

A few of the men that were with him brought me some clothing to wear. When I finished dressing, I sat at the feet of Jesus and he ministered to me. After some time, the men from my village came to see if the reports of what they had heard were true. When they saw that I was clothed and in my right mind they became afraid and pleaded with Jesus to leave their coasts. Upon hearing their plea, Jesus entered the ship to leave.

Because I knew that He was of God and in Him was truth, I desired to follow after Him. So as I started to board the ship with Him, he turned to me and said, *"Go home to your friends and tell them how great things the Lord has done for you and has had compassion on you."* And with that saying, they sailed off.

As I headed towards my village, I avowed His commandment for my life to be a witness to the power of God in my earthly home, and that I would continue in this declaration of truth until I go to my heavenly home!

PROMISE

I was forlorn and desperate. There was nothing I could do. Although I held the highest rank of Centurion in the Roman army, and was a man of great authority with an incomparable reputation, I did not possess the resources or ability to help.

He had been bed ridden for days with a high fever. His eyes were turned back and his countenance revealed that he would soon give up the ghost. Of my entire household consortium, he was the person who I relied on the most. My entire household was entrusted into his care. I loved him as a brother and trusted him with my life. I searched frantically for anyone or anything that could offer any alleviation.

This was unlike me. I took great pride in my self-reliance and self-control. From the time I was young, I meticulously planned out the day and for that matter, the course of my future. I was enthralled with being a part of the 'Imperial Army'. I believe this was spurred on in part by the gladiator games. Although gladiators were not considered to be respectable citizens, I admired them for their courage, accolades and honor they received from the crowds. Then there were the accounts of Augustus Caesar's campaigns when he was general and those of Tiberius. They conquered new territories and expanded the empire. I too wanted to be admired by my countryman as a champion and conqueror.

My family were commoners and lacked material wealth or possessions. We could not afford a formal education, but my father being somewhat educated, taught me to read and the basics in mathematics. He worked for a blacksmith forging iron into work implements. I recall visiting him at work where I would gather scrap pieces of metal and imagine that they were swords. Slashing through the air I insisted that I was a soldier fighting in a far away country in some heroic battle. My mother stayed at home caring for my younger siblings and tending to our modest home.

At the age of seventeen, against the advice of my father, I enlisted into the army. Basic training lasted four long months and was arduous to say the least. We conducted drill on the field of Mars. We ran for an hour every day. We practiced leaping, bounding and swimming. Then came the training with the various types of weaponry: The shield, bow, sling, darts, javelin and sword. We repeatedly had to march nearly fifteen leagues of rough terrain laden with heavy gear while maintaining formation integrity, all within a time limit of less than five hours. I later learned that all this training was beneficial while in pursuit of the enemy. The training enabled us to advance on the enemy and overtake them with the greatest possible speed.

After completing basic training, I was assigned to the Germania Inferior legion under the command of General Germanicus and dispatched with seven other legions to Germania. This was the area where the debacle of General Quintilius Varus took place at the hands of Germanic tribes led by the nobleman Arminius some five years prior.

Shortly after arriving, we received news that Caesar Augustus had died and of Tiberius' ascension to power. Although Tiberius was a great general, he was not well received. This news caused riotous mutiny to break out among the legions. General Germanicus was not only a good soldier, but was also a man of much promise, amicable in his disposition and very popular with the soldiers. Germanicus put down the rebellion himself and restored order. With order restored, he led us in the invasion of Germania. Here is where I experienced my first taste of war.

While standing on the front line facing the barbarians only a stone's throw away, I was filled with a gamut of emotions. Fear, anger and exhilaration were the most apparent. When the order to advance was given, my legs moved instinctually without giving it a thought. Eagerly I marched forward alongside my Centurion. The barbarians roared out as the two opposing armies closed.

As our lines collided, the action moved slowly as if I was in a dream. From my left came the forceful swing of a primitive axe. Instinctively I raised my shield, deflecting the blow and immediately countered with a forward thrust to my opponents exposed torso. The sharp sword easily penetrated his body and he instantly collapsed. I had slain my first man. At once I was filled with a sense of unbridled strength and power. But, there was no time to dwell on the moment, the battle swirled around me and I had to react or I would fall victim to the advancing enemy.

The battle raged for hours. When it was done, I stood breathing heavily covered in sweat, dirt and the blood of my enemy. What had once been chaos was now calm. Dead and wounded men lay around me in every direction. We had soundly defeated our foe. This battle had given me a sense of accomplishment and pride. I longed for the next battle, not in bloodlust, but with the overwhelming desire to fight for the honor of my General, country and family. Two days later, we engaged in another battle with the same victorious results. We continued on conquering Marsi and Bructeri on the upper Ems.

The following spring, we built a fleet of ships in the Batavians and sailed through the canal of Drusus into the countries of the Frisians and Chauci where they ultimately surrendered. At Idistaviso we encountered an army led by Arminius, the one who had defeated General Varus in the Teutoburg forest. We overcame them, forcing them back in defeat. Perhaps this was Germanicus' way of effecting retribution for Varus.

Through every conflict, I came out unscathed and found favor with my centurion because of the salient bravery and military efficiency I displayed during each battle. He often praised me for being the consummate role model for the other soldiers. Because of this, by the end of the Germania campaign, I had received a field promotion to Centurion Hastatus Posterior, leading a small centuria of my own. This was truly an honor seeing that the older more seasoned soldiers usually attained this rank.

After the defeat of Arminius, we received orders from Tiberius that remitted our advance. His orders were to vacate the area and return to Rome. I did not understand it. Why would we leave now when we have the enemy on the run and there was territory to append to the empire? Tiberius' decision was a display of his tactical genius. Once we abandoned the area, the leaderless Germanic tribes began to fight amongst themselves, dispelling any chance of a coordinated effort in the future. Also, by leaving we prevented the possibility of over extending our military resources, a situation that could leave us vulnerable.

As we neared Rome, an emissary from the city came out to meet General Germanicus and informed him of the Triumph ceremony that awaited us. A triumph ceremony had not taken place in the city for almost fifty years. This was an absolute honor to be welcomed home in such a fashion.

On the day of the ceremony we began our march just outside the Servian walls next to the Tiber River. A chariot ornate with gold, silver and wreaths was brought for Germanicus to ride in on. The 'Triumph Doors', normally closed, were opened for just such an occasion. As we entered the city, we were met by the senate and magistrates where Germanicus symbolically surrendered his command. Passing through the city we were welcomed by the deafening roar of the assembled Roman citizens and an expanse of flowers as far as the eye could see. Our procession continued on the sacred road up to Capitoline Hill to the Temple of Jupiter where a white bull was sacrificed. After the conclusion of the ritual, we were dismissed to go and celebrate in the city. After a brief visit with my parents, I immersed myself in the city's celebratory atmosphere.

Our stay in Rome was brief. Germanicus found favor with Tiberius and was granted control over the eastern part of the empire. We were soon dispatched to Hellesport to the Armenian capital Artaxata to deal with the conflict between the Parthians and Armenians.

Clashes arose from time to time, during which I ascended to my current rank of Primus Pilus, the highest-ranking Centurion. Only a few others within the army were above me in rank. I was in command of cohorts and at times legions. Because of my position, I prospered financially and was treated with honor and respect, and I had counsel with Germanicus personally in regards to military matters.

Germanicus' popularity increased and there was talk of him being heir to the throne. There was however, a price to his growing popularity. Political rivals were jealous of him and rumors of conspiracies against Germanicus began to surface. He failed to take them seriously and his disregard and overconfidence cost him his life. Just two years after arriving in Artaxata, he was poisoned. The loss was devastating and demoralizing to the men under his command. His death brought to mind my own aspirations of rising in rank. I too had shared Germanicus' mind set and political aspirations. However, with the opposing political powers in play I too could end up being the target of a conspiracy.

One month after the death of Germanicus, I left Asia, transferring to a different area and legion altogether. I assembled with the VI legion Ferrata in Galilee in the province of Judaea. This area was governed by the Tetrarch Herod Antipas.

At first I lived in the capital city of Tiberius on the west shore of the Lake Tiberius. After I was familiar with the region, I relocated to a site on the east shore overlooking the sea, not far from the small city of Capernaum.

There I had built a countryside manor. My main living quarters were on the second floor just above my storehouse. Across the courtyard were the servants' quarters. Although it had room for twenty-five, only eighteen servants resided there. They cultivated the wheat fields, cared for the horses and tended to the duties of the day.

I gave no thought to the exorbitant cost of my living expenses. I took advantage of the rich soil and had a vineyard and built a grape press for making wine. On a small parcel of land I grew wheat and barley. I also had a small bath house where I entertained guests, freely drinking the wine I produced. There were occasions when I would be gone for long intervals to inspect the ranks of soldiers at their assorted posts. For these times when I was away, I left my steward Eliezer to mind the estate.

Eliezer, a local Jewish boy, came to me as a young teenager. He had been orphaned with no other family to take him in. From the onset, he displayed a strong work ethic. He worked hard from early morning to sun down. He was eager to learn and asked only the questions he could not answer himself. He never complained and took on every task with fervor. Watching him mature into a young man, reminded me of myself and my ardor to learn as much as I could. Perhaps this was the reason we formed such a strong bond.

Eliezer elected to maintain his belief and faith in his one God. He and the other servants assembled on occasion to share their stories and say their prayers. To me it was all empty talk. I remembered the religion and philosophies I grew up with in Rome. The various superstitions associated with omens, the astrologers, soothsayers and oracles. Each different god had his own set of rituals. The final artifice that disenchanted me was the farcical 'Keeper of the Sacred Chicken'. This droll man would sacrifice a chicken, examine the entrails then determine what the best course of action would be to take. It was ludicrous and even comical that people of influence would believe him. I did not need superstitions, advice from oracles or for that matter to pray to any gods. All I needed is what I held within myself, a strong mind, a strong body and a strong will. But if Eliezer's belief in his God made him the good man that he is, that was acceptable with me.

My watchman ran to me as I headed down the road towards my home. I had been away nearly two weeks. *"My Lord"* he paused to catch his breath, *"Eliezer is very sick!"* My heart dropped. I spurred my horse hard and loped down the road to the manor. As I reached the courtyard, I dismounted my horse and handed him off to one of the waiting servants. I quickly ran to Eliezer's quarters where I saw him lying in his bed semi conscious. He was drenched in sweat and his body would occasionally twitch. This was an indication that he was possibly stricken with the Palsy. I asked the one servant that was tending to him, *"How long has he been like this?"*

He answered, *"Six days my Lord. The first two days he had uncontrollable shaking"*.

"Did you send for the physician?"

"Yes Lord, four days ago. He said the only thing we can do for him is comfort him in his torment."

I did not want to believe what I was hearing. I yelled out, *"Go and summon the physician again. NOW!"*

He departed off to Capernaum and returned a short time later with the physician. The physician examined Eliezer and reaffirmed what I had already been told. I was distraught with the thought of possibly losing him. I considered him to be family. I sat with him all night wiping his brow and trying to comfort him. In the morning his conditioned had worsened. He was unconscious and his breathing had become shallower.

One of the servants entered the room, approached me and sheepishly said, *"My Lord, there may be someone who can help."*

Bewildered, I looked up at him and replied, *"Speak."*

"There is a man whose fame has spread in the region for his ability to heal people of their infirmities."

"Who is this man?" I demanded.

"Jesus from Nazareth," He replied.

I shook my head in disgust. I had heard that this Jesus was some political activist looking for people to follow him for the purpose of bringing change to the government. I knew all about political activists and their plots and I did not want to have anything to do with them.

I answered my servant, *"No. The only thing these political beasts desire is power."*

"My Lord," he interjected, *"He is the power."*

He went on to recount many stories to me of how by his word and touch he healed many that were sick and lame. He also mentioned that he was possibly the one that was foretold of in the scriptures to be the Christ. I looked down at the waning ashen face of Eliezer and thought of all the religious drivel from my past. I thought, *'If ever there was a time for me to believe in something, the time was now'*. I was desperate.

I turned to my servant and asked, *"Where is this Jesus?"*

"He is in Capernaum."

As I entered the city of Capernaum, I earnestly looked for where Jesus was. I located a large crowd that was abuzz with activity surrounding a lone man. *'This has to be Him'*, I thought. I expeditiously made my way through the mass and nervously walked up and stood in front of him. He was not at all as I imagined. He was not adorned in fancy attire; he was simply dressed and lowly looking. As I stood there fixed on his eyes, I could feel what I perceived was truth emanating from him. I could not explain it, but this strange feeling had engulfed me and drew me in.

I reverently said, *"Lord, my servant lies sick of the palsy, grievously tormented"*.

Jesus said to me, *"I will come and heal him."*

I answered him back, *"Lord, I am not worthy that you should come under my roof; but speak the word only and my servant shall be healed. For I am a man under authority having soldiers under me. When I say to this man, 'Go', he goes; and to another, 'Come', and he comes; and to my servant, 'Do this' and he does it."*

Jesus smiled at me with his eyes. He then turned to those that were with him and stated, *"Truly I say to you, I have not found so great a faith, no, not in Israel. And I say to you, that many shall come from the east and west, and shall sit down with Abraham, Isaac and Jacob in the kingdom of Heaven. But the children of the kingdom shall be cast out into outer darkness; there shall be weeping and gnashing of teeth."*

Jesus turned back to me and said, *"Go your way; and as you have believed, so be it done to you."*

I felt peace and comfort in His presence. I slowly turned and headed back home. I was anxious to go see Eliezer.

My watchman, upon seeing me as I approached, ran at me yelling, *"Lord, Lord, Eliezer has been made whole! He is up walking around!"* He relayed to me that in one moment around the space of half an hour before, he was healed. This corresponded with the time Jesus had declared his healing.

Eliezer was there at the front door to meet me. We embraced each other and laughed with collective joy. It was so good to see him up and full of life. As we talked about the incident, he looked at me in a peculiar manner. He sensed that there was something new about me. Even I felt a change and shift in my spirit, and that I was a changed person never to be the same again. As I recounted the day's events, I realized that Jesus was no oracle or soothsayer, but that He was the genuine article. I came to apprehend that there was a God, and Jesus was somehow connected to Him. This Jesus was truth, His word was truth and I needed and wanted this truth in my life.

FORGIVEN

The front door was violently forced open, causing it to slam against the wall. The impact jogged my senses, reminding me of my illicit activity. As the angry mob of men charged into the room, my male companion and I impulsively wrestled with our clothes as we tried to put them back on. Several of the men ferociously grabbed my arms, yanked me to my feet and forced me outside while exclaiming, *"Caught in the very act!"* I could hear the man I was with asserting that he did not know I was a married woman. None the less, they hauled him to his feet and pushed him outside and onto the street where they separated us.

The throng of angry men shoved me away from my accomplice down the street while yelling out, *"Adulterer! Adulterer!"* Their expletives caused those we passed by to join in on the abasement, yelling and hissing at me. Embarrassed and humiliated by this degradation, I tried to hide my shameful face. But, there was absolutely nothing I could do or say in my defense, I was guilty.

I saw several of my accusers pick up stones as we made headlong down the street. Seeing the crowd so agitated, I feared that they would lead me straight out of the city walls and stone me to death without consulting the San Hedrin. In spite of Roman laws, it appeared that they were going to take matters into their own hands. My chaotic life had reached its climax and I wondered how a young, innocent girl from Gamala could have reached this point. As I was paraded down the street, I reflected back on my tumultuous life and questioned what had led me to this juncture.

Gamala was a fortified, hillside city in the Golan, just east of the Jordan River. I was born there and although I did not live there long, I always considered Gamala to be my home. It was the only time in my life when I felt that I was truly part of a family.

My earliest memories were of following my mother around at the age of five or six and tending to various chores around our home and in the city market place. I remember waiting with anticipation for my father to get home from work. He would pick me up in his arms and tell me how much he missed me. He worked in the nearby olive groves minding the highly valued crops. One significant memory I had was that of harvest time when the gathered olives would be hauled into the city and taken to what was to me, a colossal olive press. Hundreds of olives were dumped into the olive press where a large, heavy stone was rolled over them, squeezing out the oil. I was mesmerized by the entire process.

My father, a devoutly religious man, would attend the synagogue every Sabbath and several times throughout the week to meet with the elders and discuss the political climate. Gamala, which was in the northern province of Samaria, was overseen by the Roman appointed Jewish king Herod Archelaus. It was a hot bed when it came to discussions of the political hierarchy and the authority they exercised in governing the people.

The boiling point was reached when the Roman authorities deposed of Archelaus and appointed the new governor Coponius. Coponius tried to impose a new tax system that weighed heavily on the people and caused uproar. In response, a Pharisee named Zadok and a scribe named Judas, banded together and incited the people of the city by telling them that the taxation was comparable to slavery. They urged the people to stand for their liberty. They declared that God was Israel's only Lord and it was blasphemous to pay tribute to anyone else including the Roman emperor who some considered to be divine. They also proclaimed that 'God would be their zealous helper'. Because of this philosophy, they were labeled with the title of 'zealots'. This agitating and riling up of the people caused unrest and because of this, small insurrections periodically rose up in protest to the tax.

My father was one of those caught up in the fray against the government and was a strong opponent of the new tax. I remember my mother pleading with him not to get involved with the insurgence, but he was too emotionally involved.

My life became unglued one particular afternoon when my father did not return home from work. Word had reached us that a minor skirmish had taken place between the men of our city and the Roman soldiers. The townsmen were no match against the well armed and well trained soldiers. Three of the men from our city had been killed; my father had been one of the casualties. The news of my father's death was devastating to my mother. At the time, I did not fully understand what had happened, all I knew was that my father would never come home again.

With the absence of my father, the following year was difficult for my mother as she was barely able to eke out a living for the both of us. To add to the hardships, there was also the constant threat of retaliation from the Roman authorities.

With tensions rising and the looming threat of retribution from the Roman authorities, several families believed that the longer they remained in the city, the greater the risk would be to their livelihood. They decided that it would be propitious for them to leave Gamala. Realizing that there was no promise of conditions improving if we stayed, my mother decided it would be in our best interest if we accompanied those leaving the city.

With no living relatives on my father's side, we had only one option; live with my mother's brother in the city of Scythopolis.

Within three days of leaving Gamala, we reached the large city of Scythopolis. Because of the bustling commerce and abundance of fertile lands, the families we were traveling with, also chose to settle here.

We arrived at my uncle's home, a farm on a small parcel of land located on the outlaying area of the city. Our arrival was a surprise to my uncle and rather than receiving us with compassion, he received us with indifference. It was evident by his demeanor that he believed we were an inconvenience to him and his family and he resented us being there. In spite of the way he felt, he did not turn us away. He led us to a small shed next to a goat corral a short distance from his house. We cleared out the tools that were inside and that became me and my mother's new home. It was cramped and had little room for our beds let alone the rest of our belongings, but it provided us with much needed shelter.

The next day, my uncle immediately put us to work tending to all the animals and completing the chores associated with the upkeep of the farm. Now that he was burdened with providing for us, he regarded us as less than second class citizens. Instead of treating us like family, he behaved as if we were his personal slaves. He made us work from sun up to sun down with scarcely any time to rest. Initially, the work was difficult, but as the years passed my mother and I settled into a daily routine. And though my uncle's contempt for us did not seem to diminish, our lives became more manageable.

Just when it seemed that things were starting to get better, my life was again thrust into disarray. One day when I was barely fifteen years old, my mother, my uncle's wife and children went into town to purchase food and supplies. I remained at the farm tending to the daily chores. Shortly after they had departed, my uncle beckoned for me to come and help him move some furniture inside his home. As I entered, he immediately sprang upon me, forcing both of us to the ground. When I attempted to get up, he positioned his body atop mine using his body weight to keep me pinned down. He placed one of his hands around my throat and with the other began removing my clothing. Frightened and frantic, I tried to push him off of me. But he countered my attempts at resistance by squeezing my neck, applying crushing pressure making it difficult for me to breathe. After several unsuccessful attempts to get him off of me and filled with the fear that he would kill me, I stopped resisting his assault. I lay helpless as he held me down and forcibly raped me.

When my uncle was finished, he threatened to take all of our belongings from us and cast my mother and me out if I spoke a word to anyone about the incident. With tears pouring from my eyes, I spit in his face and immediately ran from his house across the way and into our shelter, locking the door behind me. Filled with anguish and shame, I sobbed uncontrollably as I tried to reason why he had violated me in such a way.

When my mother returned home, she saw what state I was in and immediately inquired what was wrong. I gave an account of the entire incident right down to his threats of casting us out to fend for ourselves. She embraced me and we wept together well into the evening. The next morning when I awoke, I saw my mother nervously pacing back and forth in our small shed. She was in a quandary between confronting my uncle, which would result in him casting us out to be destitute, or keeping silent, thus insuring our home and security. She chose to do the latter. I took great issue with her decision and it ultimately caused tension to arise between us. To me, her silence was a loud and clear signal that she condoned what had happened. I considered that an act of betrayal.

Because of my mother's disloyalty and the abhorrent thought of having any further contact with my uncle, I confined myself to our shed and refused to do any more work on the farm. After several weeks of isolation, I knew that I had reached a crossroads in my life. I could no longer stay in this awkward situation filled with bitterness. I had to get away and find a better way of life. At the opportune time, when everyone was working in the fields, I snuck into my uncle's house and found where he kept is money. I took all of his silver, gathered some food and immediately headed into the city before they noticed that I was gone. Once I reached the city, I knew I could not linger. If I stayed too long, it would be just a matter of time before my uncle found me and had the authorities arrest me for stealing his money. I had to leave the region all together.

Traveling alone would not be prudent. Not only would the perilous terrain be a challenge, but a lone female would present a potentially easy target for bandits to assail. After searching hastily through the city, I located grain merchants heading to Jerusalem and joined up with them.

The migration southward was long and arduous. We departed near the end of summer when it was still very hot and humid. We cut across hills and meandered through valleys. But in spite of the uncomfortable weather conditions and troublesome terrain, we pressed on for four long days until we reached Jerusalem.

I was taken aback by the beauty and splendor of the great city. I soon found out that traveling through it was no easy task. It was easy to get lost within the enormous walls and busy streets. Every street looked the same, lined with people going about their daily routines. I was fortunate that one of the grain merchants that I had traveled with was a frequent visitor to the great city and was very familiar with the area.

He guided me to an inn located on the southeast hill of the lower city. This area is where most of the poor resided in congested living conditions. This neighborhood was the only area that was affordable to me. Here, I was able to rent a small room from a keeper for a nominal price. Now that I had found someplace to stay, I was hard pressed in search of a livelihood. The silver I had taken from my uncle would not last long.

It took me a couple of days, but I was able to find work in the olive groves in the hills surrounding the city. The oil acquired from the olives was the city's biggest export and there was always a demand for workers. Working in that environment brought me some solace, as it revived memories of a past life, long ago with my father in Gamala.

Because of the endless cascade of emotions that flooded my memory on a daily basis, I threw myself into work trying to forget the past, but it was no use. Along with the resentment and shame came anger and a loss of self confidence. I isolated myself believing that I was unworthy to have any association with others. There were times when I even contemplated suicide. It seemed as though I had run away from a life of hopelessness only to step into one of despondency.

Over the next several years, I trudged through my solitary life becoming more and more cynical towards humanity. I settled into a daily rut: work, eat and sleep. When in the city, I stayed within the confines of the lower city as not to stray too far from my comfort zone. It was not much of a life. It was a destitute existence.

One day I happened to wander into an area of the upper city where I had never been before. It was as if I had been granted entry into a hidden society of an elevated culture. The upper city consisted of broad avenues and spacious homes, an absolute contrast to the packed quarters where I lived. The houses there were manors with courtyards, pools and elegant gardens which housed the rich and powerful families as well as high ranking Roman officials. Every household had several servants that attended to the daily chores.

These aristocratic homes were only outdone by the grandiose dwelling of Herod's palace. Across from his palace was the upper market, an open court consisting of vendors in booths selling their wares. I had never seen such merchandise before. There, merchants dealt in ivory, incense, and precious stones alongside gold and silver smiths, silk merchants and master tailors. Many of the foods and spices were imported and foreign to me. Only the wealthy shopped here and I was in a state of awe as I haphazardly ambled through the area.

I was drawn to an area of the market place by the sweet fragrances of perfumes I had never smelled before. I stopped in front of a booth and stood there in a hypnotic state breathing in the different aromas as they hypnotically danced around me. I was entranced by the calmative and soothing effect it had on me. My trance was broken by a man inside the booth, motioning for me approach. I was reluctant at first, but driven by my intense desire to know what smelled so good, I capitulated to his bidding.

He was an older man dressed in fine clothing and adorned with gold jewelry. Two other young men working with him were modestly dressed by comparison. He was obviously the owner. His aim was to try and sell me some expensive oil or perfume and judging by his fluent sales pitch, he was very good at his craft.

I just stood mute, shaking my head in dissent as he attempted to sell me perfume bottle after perfume bottle. Then he stopped his incessant chatter and after an abrupt pause, he stepped back and examined me from head to toe. He came to his senses and realized that I was not the type of client he thought I was. He smiled, turned away and reached back into a bag and turned back towards me. He held out a small clay jar different from the other expensive alabaster, onyx and glass jars he had previously been showing me.

He extended the jar at me and said, *"Please take it. You are a beautiful woman and you should have this."* Unsure of what to do, I just stood there staring at the jar. Helping to bolster my decision, the man said, *"It is a gift. Take it."*

I reached out and accepted his charity and without saying a word, I walked off. I found a quiet place to sit and examine the contents of the jar. It contained a rose oil perfume with an amazing odor. I excitedly dabbed a few drops onto my arm and the smell of it filled the air around me. I felt transformed and for the first time in a long while, I felt pretty. The following day, I went back to the upper city to thank the man for his wonderful and uplifting gift, but he was not there. The men that were working in his booth informed me that he would be gone for several weeks attending to his business. Slightly dispirited by his absence, I left with the hope of seeing him again.

I was frugal in the application of the rose oil and I was able to make the treasured substance in the small jar last nearly three weeks. When the container was empty, I went back into the upper market to return it and to express my appreciation.

The perfume and oil merchant was there and he was delighted to see me again. I handed him the empty jar and repeatedly thanked him for his generosity. I then apologized for my rudeness in not thanking him in the first place. I explained that I had returned the following day, but that he was away. He explained to me that he was away traveling in the Far East collecting the very expensive spikenard. He beckoned me to enter his booth and as I did, he led me towards the rear and showed me the valuable plant. It had bell shaped pink flowers and emitted a soft, sweet aroma. He described how the extract of the plant could not only be used as perfume oil, but as incense or as an herbal medicine to help people sleep.

After breathing in the spikenard and hearing about some of its properties, I was intrigued and wanted to hear and smell more. He held up a jar containing the rare oil of the persimmon. He explained that in ancient times, this oil was poured over the heads of the new king during their anointing ceremony. The fragrance was captivating. I was also exposed to the less expensive, common oils, such as orris, clove, cardamom and costus. Each one had its own unique scent.

The short time we spent together that afternoon seemed to rekindle feelings inside me that I had not felt since I was a child. When he spoke to me, it was with consideration and care. He actually looked me in the eyes, unlike others who looked past me as if I did not exist. I was enamored with the attention he was giving me. When I left that afternoon, he filled the small jar up with a different oil and bestowed to me another gift. I left with a newly discovered enthusiasm.

Over the next year, I visited him with regularity when he was not away. We grew close. Eventually our relationship began to blossom and evolved into something more meaningful. He lavished me with gifts and I was taken with the way he doted on me. Over the course of time, he asked me to marry him. Although he was much older, I felt that this was the nurturing relationship that I had been searching for all along. I consented and because I had told him that I was an orphan, which was half a truth, we were wed in a small ceremony with just a few witnesses. I moved into his intermediate sized home located in the upper city and began my new found life as his wife.

All was well at first; we were able to spend a lot of time together. But, as time passed, his priorities shifted and he was seldom around. He was either away in another country gathering goods for his oils or in the marketplace working with little or no time for me. I felt neglected and the old feelings of abandonment reemerged and I found myself lonely, desperately longing for attention.

While he was away on his adventures, I often found myself at home lonely, disinterested and bored, even though I had fine clothing, jewelry and more than I could have imagined, I was not satisfied. I wandered through the city in search of something to occupy my interest, but nothing caught my eye. Bored with Jerusalem, I ventured to the nearby surrounding small cities of Bethphage and Bethany, not knowing what I was in search of.

It was during one of these excursions to Bethany that a much younger man caught my attention. He was working in the fields, and as I walked down the road between cities, he walked alongside the entire time showering me with compliments. I pretended to be aloof and shrugged off his advances. Although others may have found his adulation frivolous, I found that it bolstered my sense of self worth.

The following day, eager for more affection, I returned to the same area purposely seeking out the young man. It did not take long. As I traveled down the road, he saw me and immediately left the field he was working in and ran to my side. This time, instead of ignoring him, I flirted back. It was invigorating to receive this kind of attention from someone. I continued meeting the young man well into the following week. Our meetings grew more emotionally intense. We began to step over the bounds of physical love that were meant to be shared only between a husband and wife. I eventually gave into my passions and we were sexually intimate. I knew this illicit romance was wrong, but the way he made me feel wanted and appreciated overrode my feelings of guilt.

Over the span of two weeks, the affair continued and grew more fervid until my husband returned home. During this time, I stopped seeing the young man but eagerly anticipated our next meeting. Within two weeks my husband was off again, traveling to some far off land in search of some 'exotic fragrance'. The day after he left, I rushed to see my secret bedmate. When I found him, he was standoffish. He told me that he wanted nothing more to do with me and that we were finished. I did not understand why he was so curt. I ran home heartbroken trying to make sense of the situation. In time, I became remorseful for what I had done. I was married, and even though my husband was not around, I felt the conviction that he cared for me deeply. In the following months after my adulterous tryst, the relationship between my husband and I did not improve. In fact it worsened. His travels became more frequent, leaving me at home to deal with my feelings of alienation.

In the course of time, when my husband was away, again the compulsion to roam into the neighboring cities arose and I found myself seeking something or someone who would provide me with the acceptance that I so desperately wanted. I met different men, who at first asserted their approval and concern, which was appealing to me. The start of each romance was exhilarating and I welcomed the intimacy. But after each man got what they wanted out of the liaison, the relationship ended in disappointment. It was the same in every situation, only the faces changed. I hoped with each relationship that maybe this one would be the one that would provide me with the validation I was in need of. But each one failed to reach my expectations.

My behavior became more daring in that I was not only visiting the other cities, but I began conducting my promiscuous activity within Jerusalem. I was unable stop my destructive behavior. I carried on with total disregard, running the risk of getting caught. I believe deep down inside I wanted to get caught. I was tired of the deception and fruitless searching. I needed help, but who could I turn to?

And now, having been finally caught, I felt a sense of relief despite being terrified about the possible outcome.

There was no doubt I had ruined my life, but there was no telling how many other lives I had negatively affected by my selfish and depraved acts.

As we marched down the streets, the barely controlled throng grew even larger as they continually announced my sin. To my relief, we were not headed towards any of the gates leading out of the city. We were headed towards the Temple. It appeared they were going to take me to the San Hedrin for judgment after all. Not that this would be any more beneficial to my plight, it would only delay the inevitable.

As we approached the Temple, I could see the white stone platform that it was built upon. At the entry there was a small gathering of Pharisees and Scribes. When we approached, the angry mob informed them of my offense. The religious leaders then led us into the outer court and shoved me in front of Jesus who at the time was speaking to the people. The men encircled me as I stood alone in the midst.

I had heard him speak once before. He claimed to be the Son of God. I heard stories of people being miraculously healed, but had yet to see it for myself. I believed he was just one of many trying to gain followers by claiming he was the messiah. The one time I heard him speak, I thought about confronting him and asking why God failed to protect my father or why He did not protect me from my uncle or the other men who had used me. No, he was probably just another philosopher claiming to have all the answers. I was somewhat baffled however as to why the Pharisees and Scribes brought me before him. They practically despised him themselves.

Then they spoke to him as if accusing him, *"Master, this woman was taken in adultery, in the very act! Now Moses in the Law commanded us that she should be stoned. But what do you say?"*

Jesus did the strangest thing. Acting as if he did not hear them, He stooped down and placed his finger against the cobble stone pavement and began to write. As I watched him do this, there was something familiar with his actions, but I could not figure out what it was.

The men continued to urge him to answer until he stood up and faced them. Then he answered, *"He that is without sin among you, let him first cast a stone at her."*

I thought, *"Why isn't he casting judgment on me? I am guilty."* Again he stooped down and wrote on the ground. It was then that my eyes were opened and my heart fell within me. I now knew why this was so familiar to me.

Thoughts of the past of when I was a young girl were instantly brought to remembrance. I recalled a specific day when my father returned home from synagogue and began to share some of the scriptures with me. He chronicled the time Moses had received the Law. He told me that when Moses had been given the two stone tables of testimony, that they had been written with the finger of God not once, but twice.

As I watched Jesus' finger write on the cobble stone pavement for the second time, I had a revelation: The only one who can truly judge according to the Law is the one who decreed it. His statement and actions were loud and clear: He knows the Law because He wrote it and gave it to us – therefore, He is the Son of God! Standing there in amazement, I noticed that my accusers began to leave one by one until just the two of us remained.

My heart was filled with conviction and I was genuinely repentant for the sin in my life. Jesus stood up and looked at me. With my eyes affixed on His, I waited for Him to pass righteous judgment on me.

"Woman," He asked me, *"Where are those that accuse you? Is there no man to condemn you?"*

I answered, *"No man, Lord."*

With forgiveness in his voice, He replied, *"Then neither do I condemn you. Go and sin no more."*

In that moment a transformation took place in my heart. I realized that He not only shielded me from my accusers, but had protected me from continuing in the lifestyle that lead down the road to destruction. Instead of judgment and condemnation, He had given me His forgiveness, favor and love that I was undeserving of. He had filled that empty void inside of me and forever I would belong to Him.

REDEEMED

I sat there alone on the cold hard ground of my prison cell contemplating the events that landed me here. Anger welled up inside of me and I cursed out loud. But the anger did not last long. With the sun beginning to set and the temperature dropping as day turned to night, my anger turned to resignation, which seemed to put me at ease for a while. But, realizing the truth of my tenuous hold on life, I was overwhelmed by grief and wept into my hands.

With the incident playing over and over again in my head, I thought, *'Why did I do it? If I had just kept walking by, I would be safe somewhere else and with many more days of life to look forward to'*. But, having been arrested three days ago by Roman soldiers and sentenced, I was to die on the marrow at the age of twenty six.

With the masses coming to Jerusalem from all over the region for the observance of Passover, the city was teeming with diverse people. Many were at the Temple to worship and pay their taxes. The number of Roman soldiers had been increased around the Temple because of the swelling assemblage. This was done to monitor and deter any activity that would pose a threat to Roman power.

While strolling through the Temple courtyard by one of the tables where taxes were being collected, I saw the open bag of the tax collector. It was filled with beautiful silver coins bearing the emperor's image and avarice gained the better of me.

It happened so fast and I just reacted! The man in front of me reached over the table and grabbed at the open bag of coins. A struggle over the bag ensued between he and the tax collector. The bag tore open and coins flew everywhere. The man grabbed a hand full and ran off. Caught up in the excitement, I also grabbed a handful of coins, trapped them against my chest, turned and ran. Those around yelled out, *"Thief! Someone stop him! He's a thief!"* I ran less than twenty steps before I was abruptly surrounded by four Roman soldiers with the tip of their swords and spears pointed at me. I let the coins fall to the ground and I was immediately arrested and imprisoned. Apparently, two of the guards had witnessed the entire incident. This thwarted my success from the outset since my escape plan was non-existent. The other man had gotten a lot further before he was eventually captured. Our trial was brief and to the point. Because of the Roman soldiers' testimony, we were thought to be working in concert with each other. The truth was I did not know the other man. None the less, we were found guilty and sentenced to be crucified.

I suppose it was payment for my bent and dishonest existence up to this point. I had stolen many times before and was crafty in my dealings with others. If I had to cheat or steal for gain, I did it with no contrition. Now in my penitence, I believe my depraved, past criminal life had caught up to me.

My prison cell was basically a small cave in the rock. It was cold, dank and smelled of death which seemed to magnify my solitude. At our sentencing, I remember looking at the other man and placing the blame on him for my predicament. I recalled seeing him in the city on several occasions. He was older than me, maybe by ten years. His face had a hardened look and his eyes bore no emotion. His clothes were worn and he was caked in dirt. It became apparent to me that his full intention of visiting the Temple courtyard that day was to take advantage of whatever opportunity was presented to him. He was a life-long criminal and I wondered how he became that way.

As I spent time in my cell thinking about him, I realized that he was a personification of the man I would have become in ten years time. I was on the same road he was on. Although my heart was not yet entirely calloused and I still had some compassion for others, I could see that if I was to keep on the same heading, I would eventually end up being just as cruel, merciless and indifferent as this man. I had, without a doubt chosen the wrong path to follow and had made a mess of my life. With my eyes now opened to this, my heart was heavy and filled with regret.

I was awakened by the distant crowing of a rooster. At first I was disoriented, then remembered the gravity of my situation. Over the next hour or so just before daybreak, I could not stop thinking of what the day had in store for me. I was scared. My heart felt as though it had fallen into the pit of my stomach and the strength in my body left me. *'I don't want to die.'*

Shortly after the sun had risen, the soldiers came and retrieved both the other man and me from our cells. There, on the ground lay two wooden beams. They ordered us to each pick one up and carry it. This however, was no easy task. They were very heavy and the beam pressed deeply into my back and shoulders putting tremendous strain on my legs.

As we left the prison which was near the Antonia fortress, we were immediately joined by another man that was also carrying a beam like ours. He was a bloody mess and had great difficulty walking. His face was heavily bruised, portions of his beard had been plucked out and his eyes were nearly swollen shut. His body was drenched in blood and as a man, he was unrecognizable.

I noticed that his head bore a circlet of long thistles embedded deep into his skin. Judging by his appearance, coupled with the thorns on his head, I concluded that he had been a victim of the "king game" better known as basilinda. This was the game that roman soldiers sometimes played on condemned prisoners. The cruelty involved the soldiers' competitively rolling dice to see who would be given the right to sarcastically treat the prisoner like a king. This was done with hostile intent and was meant to mock and degrade the condemned.

As we walked through the city, a large crowd followed, bellowing out insults at us, The principal target of these insults was the bloodied man. That is when I learned from those jeering in the crowd that this man was Jesus. *'How could it be?'* I thought. *'This is Jesus the miracle worker?'* I had heard him speak before. He was a peaceful man who had preached repentance throughout the region. I even saw him give sight to a blind man. He claimed to be the Son of God. What could he have possibly done to end up here in the same circumstance as me?

Along the way, the people began to spit and cast stones at us. This ridicule and humiliation magnified our physical torment. A short distance through the city, Jesus fell to the ground and could no longer carry His beam. The soldiers forcibly grabbed an onlooker from the crowd and ordered him to pick up and carry the beam the rest of the way. We continuously had to stop as Jesus in His weakened state, would periodically collapse to the ground.

They led us just outside of the city gate and stopped at the location they called 'The Place of a Skull', right alongside one of the main thoroughfares leading to and from the city. At this place, there were wooden beams already sticking up vertically with their bases fixed in the ground. Upon reaching these, the soldiers ordered us to drop our wooden beams on the ground. After we did as we were told and rid the crosspieces from our backs, we were given gall to drink. The taste was bitter and I did everything I could to swallow and keep it down. I knew that the gall would give me some relief from the pain I was to bear, so I boldly asked for more to drink. Instead, they stripped me of my clothing and ordered me to lie on my back on top of the beam I had just dropped. Knowing what was coming next, I refused. Two of the soldiers grabbed me and forced me to the ground. I tried resisting with all the strength I had, but I could not overcome the weight and strength of these well-trained men.

They stretched my right arm out to line up with the beam. One of the soldiers who had already been there waiting for us, pulled out a long iron spike and placed the point of it against my hand. I could feel the sharp point pressing against my skin at the fringe of penetration. He raised a hammer in preparation to strike.

"Please! Please! Don't do this", I begged him.

He gave me a quick glance and smirked. Then, with one swift forceful motion, he struck the spike causing it to pierce through my entire hand and partially bury itself in the underlying wood. For an instant there was nothing, and then the excruciating searing pain shot through my hand an arm. From there, it resonated through every nerve in my body. I yelled out as loud as I could as tears poured uncontrollably from my eyes. I yelled out, *"Please, no!"* The soldier continued with six more powerful strikes until the head of the spike was resting against my hand.

Waves of nausea rolled through my bowels. I began to sweat and fade in and out of consciousness. With the tremendous shock of pain surging through my body, they stretched out my other hand with no resistance and drove a spike through it, thus firmly attaching my hands to the beam. I struggled to catch my breath as I lay there under the warm sun, staring into the cloudless sky, in total disbelief of what was happening.

The soldiers hoisted and secured the beam I was nailed to onto one of the fixed, vertical beams, forming a cross. I could feel the warm blood seeping out of my hands and rolling slowly along my now trembling forearms. Now upright, the soldiers placed my right foot atop my left, bent my legs and twisted the trunk of my body towards the left. They fastened a block of wood at the bottom in support of my feet, and then a spike was driven into both of my feet attaching them to the beam. I yelled out as the intense pain flooded the lower part of my body. I gasped, trying desperately to breathe as my body writhed in search of any possible position that would provide relief from the pain. But, it was to no avail.

My arms felt as though they were slowly separating away from my shoulders. The strain placed on my upper body made breathing practically impossible. I could breathe in, but could not fully breathe out unless I pushed up on my feet. But doing this put tremendous pressure on my feet causing burning, unbearable pain. This viscous cycle repeated itself over and over. The weight and pressure exerted on my legs caused cramping and uncontrollable shaking throughout the rest of my body. After a period of time there was some numbness in my hands and feet. However, the extreme pain was unyielding as was the difficulty in catching my breath. Only my fear of death kept me struggling to breathe in spite of my suffering.

My cohort had a different attitude towards the soldiers as they drove the spikes into his hands. He cursed and taunted them without relent as they hoisted him up. Even when they hammered the spike through his feet, he did not yield in his harassment towards them. In spite of his pain and driven by his hate, he continued to revile and spit at them.

The soldiers then came to Jesus and stripped him of his clothes. The flesh on His back was ripped open like that of a slaughtered animal. Having seen this sight before, it was apparent that the Roman soldiers had flogged him. It was hard to believe that after being beaten and flogged that he was still alive. I was confounded by his apparent lack of resistance; he lay on his back and willingly stretched out his arms against the wooden beam. It seemed as if the entire scene had been choreographed or maybe it was because he was just too exhausted to put up a fight.

When they hammered the spikes into His hands, he cried out in agony. I cringed as they drove each spike into his hands. When they hoisted him up between us, all he did was groan and gasp for air. The sound caused by the nailing of his feet to the wood, seemed only to intensify my pain.

Those who were passing by on the road looked upon us in disgust, shaking their heads. By this time, the crowd had grown, as had the severity of the cruel remarks directed at Jesus. The taunting only grew more denigrating as time went on. My cohort and I joined in with the crowd and taunted Jesus. Deep down I did not want to do this. Maybe I did this because I knew my life was about to end and I was scared. Or maybe I was hoping that by being in accord with the crowd, they would have a change of heart and release me. Whatever the reason, I knew in my heart that I was wrong and was deeply sorry for the things that I had said to him.

My circumstance caused me to profoundly reflect on my situation and I now came to the understanding that he was genuinely the Son of God. Up to this point in my life, I had rejected the truth. I was regretful for the way I lived my life. There was only one option and that was to repent. Even though I had literally reached the end of my life, if it was possible, I needed to turn from my ways. But I wondered if it was too late.

My cohort continued reviling Jesus taunting him saying, *"If you are truly the Christ . . . save yourself and us!"* His remarks were out of line and I had to speak up.

I mustered as much strength as I could and yelled back at him, *"Do you not fear God, seeing that we are in the same condemnation . . . and justly so? . . . We received our due rewards for our deeds. But this man . . . has done nothing wrong."*

I looked at Jesus with repentance and belief in my heart. I asked, *"Lord, . . remember me . . . when you come into your kingdom."*

With dried blood covering his battered face, Jesus slowly looked over at me pausing with each gasp and said, *"Truly . . . I tell you today . . . you . . . will be with me . . . .in paradise."*

Upon finishing this saying, I felt peace engulf my soul and I was no longer afraid.

Soon after, the sky grew dark and would not give way to the light. This was an abnormal occurrence for the middle of the day. A look of great concern had now overtaken the faces of onlookers and quieted their reviling. The darkness continued for several hours, during which time the strength in me had diminished to the point that I lost control of my bowels, adding to my abasement.

Continually struggling in my distressed state, I heard Jesus utter, *"Forgive them Father, ... for they do not know what they do!"*.

A short while later He cried out with a loud voice, *"Father, . . . into your hands . . . I commend my spirit."*

After hearing this, I looked over at him and saw that he had died. Immediately, the ground shook with great force and caused many to run off. I saw the centurion in charge look up at Jesus' dead body. He went down to his knees and as tears formed in his eyes, he said, *"Truly this man was the son of God!"*

As evening was drawing near, I saw a soldier use a wooden club to strike the legs of my cohort. With his legs now broken, he could no longer keep his body up making it nearly impossible to draw breath. When they got to Jesus, they pierced the side of His lifeless body with a spear to ensure that he was already dead. I knew that I would be next. Just as well, I was nearly out of strength and my fear of dying had vanished. I had been filled with a joy that was beyond words. Finally I was at peace for the first time in my life and had been assured with the hope of eternal life with God.

The soldier was now at my feet and was raising the club to strike my legs. It will not be too much longer now . . .

NOTA BENE

Nota Bene is a Latin phrase that means "note well". It is usually placed at the end of a book much like that of a postscript as an addendum or commentary on the contents of the book. If the term was to be translated today in the English, it would mean "take notice" or "pay attention".

After reading all of the stories, you may have "taken notice" and grasped the common fiber that binds each of them together. Every person carried a burden consisting of a physical ailment and/or experiencing mental and spiritual emptiness. They were liberated of their respective burdens when they encountered God's grace through Jesus.

The Merriam-Webster dictionary defines Grace (as it pertains to God): *1. unmerited help given to people by God; 2. freedom from sin through divine grace; 3. a virtue coming from God; 6. a temporary respite (as from the payment of a debt).*

I have also heard others describe grace as undeserving forgiveness and mercy or unmerited favor and love. I think the best explanation of what God's Grace is, was this analogy that I once heard:

A friend comes to me and asks if he can borrow my car for the day to run errands. I hand over the keys and he leaves. During his travels, he is involved in a non-injury automobile accident resulting in the totaling of my vehicle. I respond to the scene, view the mess and learn that he was one hundred percent at fault due to reckless and irresponsible negligence.

Now I have several options. I could be irate and bawl him out for his irresponsible behavior, straining our relationship or perhaps causing our ties to be severed, ending our friendship. An alternative response would be to put my arm around him and with compassion and kindness, tell my friend that I am glad he is not hurt and that I forgive him. This reaction would be equivalent to that of mercy.

I would venture to say that most people who were involved in this scenario would have a reaction that falls somewhere between these two examples. But this third alternative response might help reveal the true characteristics of what grace is.

Upon responding to the scene of the accident and learning about his reckless behavior, I put my arm around my friend, tell him that I forgive him, and then take him to a car dealership where I buy him a brand new car. After that, I treat him to dinner at a five star restaurant.

This third scenario although atypical, may be humanly possible, but is highly improbable. Grace cannot be properly put into the context of earthly understanding and appears to be beyond our comprehension. To begin to understand the attributes of Grace, we have to realize that it is not an earthly concept but an abundance of unearned love that can only come from God. We can find many verses in the bible that attest to this. The most famous of these is in the Gospel of John.

John 3:16 has the distinction of being one of the most quoted and well known verses. In this verse Jesus testifies of God's Grace towards man. It reads:

For God so loved the world, that he gave His only begotten Son, that whosoever believes in Him should not perish, but have everlasting life.

Jesus states that God loves us. He does not imply that receiving His love is contingent on being a good person or that it is merited upon some good deed or actions, but that it is granted to all without restriction. His love for us was manifested in that he freely gave his Son that through Him we can be redeemed. When Jesus went to the cross He exchanged places with us. He took our sin and punishment and we in turn were covered by His righteousness entitling us to all the blessings of God.

Each person's story in this book was written with the purpose of illustrating their solitude and emptiness and God's willingness, as a result of his grace, to fill that void. This was done in the expectation of showing the similarity between the past and our lives today. Although the accounts of their lives before they met Jesus are fictional, we know that throughout recorded time, human nature remains the same. The characteristic traits of pride, greed, self-centeredness, and others that existed two thousand years ago exist today. As the author of Ecclesiastes wrote *"There is nothing new under the sun,"* we too have the same traits and live through similar ordeals of suffering loss, experiencing heartache or are dealing with unfavorable health issues.

Examining the circumstances of the people in the stories, we see that as they went about their daily lives they were misinformed about God, unaware or unknowing of His love, or plainly just rejected the involvement of God in their life. It was not until they had hit rock bottom and came to their senses that they realized they needed change.

When they encountered Jesus, they were unworthy and undeserving of receiving God's love and Jesus would have been justified in rejecting them and sending them away. But each person realized that the change they were seeking had to originate inwardly from within their hearts. There had to be a change in their thoughts, attitude and behavior concerning the demands of God for right living. With this realization they came to Jesus seeking mercy, but instead Jesus administered grace.

The same is true today. Many out there are uninformed and unknowing of God's love. As a result, they want nothing to do with the "God thing". They are preoccupied with their everyday lives unaware that God is there (at times chasing after them) waiting for them to come to Him. Unfortunately as they continue down their own errant path, it may take a series of unfavorable events to bring them to their right mind. Even then, many will still reject the free gift that is offered to them through Jesus. The truth is that Jesus could not love us any more than He already does. Aversely, He cannot love us any less. But, he will never force His love on us; we have to willingly accept it. Not accepting His love is analogous to a dear friend or family member giving us a birthday present and instead of receiving and opening it, we say thank you and leave it where it lays never unwrapping it. By doing this, we will never experience the benefits of that gift.

As my walk with God continues, I am continually growing in the knowledge of what this little word "grace" really means. I have learned that He loves me unconditionally and His mercy is new everyday. Because He remembers my sin no more, I am supplied with peace, comfort and outfitted with the hope of eternity. It is the power of God which provides freedom from sin. It is always abounding (never ending steady supply) with more than I could ever need. It is through Jesus that His grace is sufficient for all my needs even in my weakness. And most of all, through His grace I have a righteous and blameless standing before God.

One of my favorite chapters to read that describes God's grace is Psalms 103. I believe that this wonderful chapter depicts the character and desire of God's love that He has in regards towards us all.

As I mentioned before in the preface, there was an after thought that came to mind during the composing of this

book. If you were "paying attention" you have most likely already discerned that the theme of the book has to do with grace. Keeping with the theme, I am sure that you probably caught the word "GRACE" in the book's title: **G**od's
Riches
At
Christ's
Expense

But, I wonder if you caught the way in which the stories were constructed and the pattern of their arrangement? Although it was done deliberately by design, I must confess that it may have been a far fetched notion. By now I hope that your curiosity is stirred. So allow me to explain and lay some ground work. Then you can decide for yourself.

In 1772, English poet and clergyman John Newton penned one of the most acclaimed hymns known today. Published in 1779, Amazing Grace has become so prolific in that it has continued to advance the message of God's love and help transform lives. The anthem is almost immediately recognizable to believers and non-believers alike, as it is sung in church, worship services and funerals. It has become an icon in American culture.

Newton's story is amazing in itself. A foul mouthed sailor involved in the slave trade, was transformed after his life of rebelliousness against God reached its crescendo during a stormy night at sea. The words that he wrote were an expression of joy to the saving grace God had granted him despite the contemptible life he had led.

As of date, many others have added their own verses to the song as a testimony and expression of thankfulness to how their souls have been delivered through the mercies of God.

Even though there are so many more, the following are the most accepted verses that are sung today:

1 *Amazing Grace, how sweet the sound,*
That saved a wretch like me...
I once was lost but now am found,
Was blind, but now I see.

2 *T'was Grace that taught my heart to fear.*
And Grace, my fears relieved.
3 *How precious did that Grace appeared...*
the hour I first believed.

4 *Through many dangers, toils and snares*
we have already come.
T'was Grace that brought us safe thus far...
and Grace will lead us home.

5 *The Lord has promised good to me...*
His words my hope secures.
6 *He will my shield and portion be...*
as long as life endures.

7 *Yea, when this flesh and heart shall fail,*
and mortal life shall cease,
I shall possess within the veil,
a life of joy and peace.

When we've been here ten thousand years...
bright shinning as the sun.
We've no less days to sing God's praise...
then when we've first begun.

As you can see, there are numbers in the margin to the left of each verse with the exception of the last one. These numbers correspond with the chapters in the book. Each chapter's story is written to coincide to their respective verse. The last verse however, has no chapter because it speaks of the glorious future when believers will reign with Jesus forever. Until then, It is comforting to know that the same God's grace that was present two thousand years ago is still freely available to us today.

Lastly, by combining the titles of each chapter, there is the account that we live in darkness, despised in a fallen state filled with fear, but through God's promise we have been forgiven and redeemed.

And with all that, I will leave you with this thought: No matter how far one will run away from God, if they were to stop and turn around, they would be only one step away from receiving His Grace!

NOTES

Chapter 1
This story is centered around the event depicted in the Gospel of John chapter nine.

Chapter 2
This story is centered around the events depicted in the Gospel of Matthew chapters seven and eight.

Chapter 3
This story is centered around the events depicted in the Gospels of Matthew chapter nine; Mark chapter five and Luke chapter eight.

Chapter 4
This story is centered around the events depicted in the Gospels of Matthew chapter eight; Luke chapter eight and Mark chapter five.

Chapter 5
This story is centered around the events depicted in the Gospels of Matthew chapter eight and Luke chapter seven.

Chapter 6
This story is centered around the event depicted in the Gospel of John chapter eight.

Chapter 7
This story is centered around the events depicted in the Gospels of Matthew chapter twenty-seven; Mark chapter fifteen; Luke chapter twenty-three and John chapter nineteen.

Nota Bene

*T*he definition of Grace was taken from The Merriam-Webster Dictionary (2004).

The analogy of Grace was heard from a Christian broadcasted radio program many years ago.

Information about John Newton was acquired from Wikipedia, the free encyclopedia.

www.ingramcontent.com/pod-product-compliance
Ingram Content Group UK Ltd.
Pitfield, Milton Keynes, MK11 3LW, UK
UKHW041949230426
12048UKWH00008B/227